MAKE ME, BREAK ME

A RIPPTON U ENEMIES TO LOVERS ROMANCE

RIPPTON CREATIVES

SOFIA AVES

MAKE ME,
BREAK ME

a Rippton U enemies to lovers romance

SOFIA AVES

First Edition

PAPERBACK ISBN 978-1-922448-96-5

EBOOK ISBN 978-1-922448-95-8

CONTENT WARNING

This work contains graphic violence, gun violence, murder, morally gray and morally black characters, power plays, OM/other man drama (by design—it's both brief and forgivable, Nelson never intended to hurt anyone, it was a sacrifice play), recounting of trauma, explicit sexual scenes and language.

Epilogue Two (Falcon) includes BDSM, MM, menage and anal sex.

Please read safely.

For all the Friday night friends of convenience who we love to hate not to date but return to week after week anyway.

This is for you.

CHAPTER ONE

ZINZI

A warm, hard body at my back woke me out of my doze. Spooning me.

Fuck. I fell asleep. Again.

That was the problem with Dex Breaker—he was too damn cuddly. Who knew all that oversized muscle was good for more than climbing him every time I got horny once every seven days or so? I mean, he was damn good fun. My Friday night toy on demand knew exactly where to find my orgasm button and just how many times to push it.

But he also knew my rules: get out before the sun came up.

No sleepovers, like ever.

Screw the Rippton U dormitory rulebook; we used my playbook, and mine alone.

I rolled into his warmth, pressed both hands to his rock hard pecs, and gave a push. "Out. Get *out*, Dex. Of. My. Damn. Bed." I kept on pushing until I rolled him to the edge of the mattress and tipped him off.

Thud.

"Fuck me, Zin. You play too rough." His gravelly voice did super fun things to my swollen pussy lips, the shape of him seared into my depths. Recently, too.

Not to mention the cute-as-all-get-out sleepy eyes and mussed hair that still had my finger tracks in its curls.

All that gave me tugs in the heart strings department which was why sleepovers with Dex were a great big, red flagged, no-fucking-*NO*.

"I have a rep for breaking my toys," I acknowledged, listening to the silence around us. The dorm was either empty—unlikely, midterm—or it was really damn late and I'd come too close to breaking my own rules. "Friday night's over. Get out of my room. I need to sleep."

Dex crashed back to the floor with a groan at

whatever he read on my face. "I'll sleep with you, babe."

I poked my head over the edge of the bed, my black hair tumbling haphazardly over my face in the dim reflected light from the union quadrangle outside my shitty little college room window. God alone knew what I looked like. Well, him and Dex.

"I'm not going to fall asleep with you or anyone else," I hissed.

"On the contrary, you just did. And your tiny snores are cute as hell. More like purrs, really." He winked at me, his come-hither, sexy ass smile curving sinful lips.

Sinful, because I knew just how much havoc that devious mouth could wreak on my body. Hell, I still bore evidence of his personal style, marks that I'd touch whenever the urge hit me midweek, reminding myself of the way he played us both into blissful oblivion.

"You're not leaving." I rolled onto my back and covered my face with my hands, leaving my body naked and exposed. It wasn't like he hadn't seen everything before, anyway. "Why aren't you leaving?"

"Because I know what I can do with that stunning fucking body of yours if you let me stay." Dex got up on his knees and leaned over me to kiss me upside down.

His tongue invaded my mouth, tasting of him and me together because the slick bastard liked to lick me to one last orgasm once we were done for the night. He *always* had to have the last word.

Fine. If he wanted to play dirty, I'd play dirty. I kissed him back, lacing my fingers through his hair and scratched his scalp the way I knew he loved. I knew everything about what Dex Breaker liked, but he forgot that in my hands, that knowledge was a weapon for me to abuse.

I drew back just enough to lick his bottom lip. "Get going, or I'll cancel next Friday."

He broke the remnants of our last kiss and stared down at me in abject horror. "You wouldn't dare, you little hell cat. You know my Friday fuck sesh with you is the one highlight I can't go without. There's nothing like a boring week in the law department to make up new ways to torture that tight little body of yours."

"Oh, I will," I promised him, licking my lips. "Now get your sexy ass out my door before you break my rule."

Dex wrinkled his nose. "You and your fucking

rules, sweetness," he grumbled. "The fuck did my pants go?"

I rolled over to unhook his pants from one corner of my bed and tossed them at him. "Shirt's over the bathroom door," I said helpfully, not moving any further than I needed.

"We got raunchy huh, girl?" He pulled his shirt over his head and yanked his jeans on from where they puddled near the door.

We never made it far before we got naked and filthy, in every sense. Dex made good work of my body. I'd be tender as hell come tomorrow morning. Endorphins still coursed through me at high speed, leaving my legs liquid and my body floating. Which was kind of the point of our Friday night catch ups.

I sighed as I ran my hands down my body. Yup, Dex knew how to show a girl a good time. I'd remember his fuck session right through to next weekend when we'd do it again and again. Every single Friday night, like clockwork. Or was that cockwork? The man fucked me into a brainless state. And now he needed to leave so I could function for the rest of the week.

Despite my determination to be alone my fingers traced through the mess he'd left on my stomach and thighs. How many times had he come on me?

And inside me? The man had endless endurance. The sigh became a moan as I touched my swollen, over-sensitized clit. All movement at the door stopped as I played with myself.

"Fuck, that's hot," Dex rumbled in the sort of tone that indicated the randy law student was ready to go again.

Good feelings gone.

"Out, out, *out*." I threw both my pillows at him without looking at what I aimed to hit.

Dex laughed as he opened my door. "Sweet dreams, Zin. Thanks for the night of debaucherous fucking sin." He laughed his ass off down the hall, apparently proud of his shitty little ditty—see, I could do it too—and likely woke the whole dorm.

Fuck them. I needed sleep, and I needed it now. My head slapped the mattress before I remembered I'd thrown my pillows at Dex and the tall, muscular shit hadn't thrown them back.

Fuck my life.

CHAPTER TWO

DEX

Friday never came around fast enough for my liking. One night a week with Zin left a lot of evening hours open. I could lie to myself and say that was why I took up illegal cage fighting on the weekends after I saw her, but the truth was that every night without Zinzi in my arms and my bed was a cruel sort of torture. That, and she still hadn't twigged that I was so bored with my coursework that I didn't spend my nights studying or cramming come exam week, unless it was to design new ways to make her come.

I got an extra payout for each fight I won—and I never went into the cage with the intent to lose. Plus, weekend fights meant I was mostly healed by the time I saw her again the following Friday when we bounced like bunnies without the reproduction issue to ruin the afterglow.

And what an afterglow. Zinzi Jones fucked like a champ, sucked like a pro, and snored like a kitten. I wanted to keep her in my bed, in my arms, and the fuck away from the rest of Rippton U's over indulgent student population who ogled her glossy black locks and slim frame at least as often as I did. Miles of long, creamy legs she usually tucked into biker boots and skin tight dark jeans I got the honor of peeling from her delicious fucking body once a week that were destined for my eyes only.

Twice, if I didn't piss her off the way I had tonight.

I blew out a sharp breath and rolled onto my back, already hard enough to rub one out at the memory of her clenching, soaked pussy wrapped around my cock. I fisted my length, pumping once, but it was no good. If it wasn't her, I couldn't. Not after the night we'd had. My head hit my pillow—not hers—and I groaned aloud.

"Oi! Get all fucking lovelorn with your chick, not in my fucking ear!" One of my roommates, a Brit called Nelson who claimed some rank or other in the House of Lords, slammed his fist into the other side of our thin, adjoining bedroom walls.

"Fuck off," I grumbled.

My mutter wasn't loud enough for him to hear, but he was right. I should have gotten all my jollies out on Zin—or in Zin. Hell, in my frame of mind I could try for open mike night at the local college bar on a Monday evening for shits and giggles.

"You're funny," Nelson muttered on the other side of my paper thin wall, though I knew he hadn't heard my not-so-witty repartee.

Too thin walls for an extravagant, billionaire-offspring-worthy-only college like Rippton U that was situated in its own freaking town in eastern California. Hell, maybe I should have pledged for a frat, but halfway through my second year, I really didn't have the energy to give a fuck. Only for Zin.

Ignoring my roomie's outburst and glad my third was away on his super yacht getting his own jollies out with his current crush and fighting with his mafia daddy—his real one—I palmed my cock for a second attempt. It was all too easy to recall the feel of Zin's soft but strong body beneath mine, the way her eyes glowed as she came, my name wrapped up in her lips like a fucking Christmas bow months too early.

Even when I rubbed myself raw twice over, sleep evaded me.

A scarred fist came flying at my face, followed in short order by a poorly timed kick. I ducked both, avoiding my opponent's roundhouse that missed me by the proverbial mile. I didn't even have to dance backward though I bounced on my toes to keep my energy up anyway. He tired fast while I still danced around the heavyset motherfucker, tracking him across the cage floor and wearing him out for the hell of it. He stumbled a step and his next lunge was more in the realm of haymaker than jab.

Good.

I ducked his next two wide swipes, dropping one shoulder in a fake to earn myself an opening. The big guy followed my lead into the feint. I clocked the side of his head with a sharp elbow that sent him sprawling forward onto the sweat and blood stained floor in an uncontrolled drop. Just to make sure he didn't get up again to haunt me, I planted a knee and a second elbow into his back.

Banging his forehead against the cement floor finished him off, his body limp at my feet. Blood splattered the concrete from the dude's broken nose, but I managed not to get any of it on me.

The ref gave me a thumbs up from the outside of

the cage, the chicken shit, while the crowd roared my name. One more scratch on the post beneath my initials, alongside the maniacs who fought before me, but I was fast catching the olds in terms of body count.

It wasn't like there'd be any evidence left for the police to find to screw with my future in law if they finally managed to get wind of the operation. I suspected that Jericho, the local fight organizer, paid several of the dirtier uniforms enough to look the other way a few times a week, as well as for a few side gigs I actively avoided. The whole place was temporary, and everything would be ash before the cops had a chance to investigate.

My name echoed around the bloodstained arena. It still didn't sound as pretty as when Zin said it, swathed in sweat and clenching my cock with her hot little pussy. I kept the image of her beneath me in my mind as I laced my fingers through the cage's metal exoskeleton. Giving the rusty wire a shake, I played up to the crowd until they screamed my name louder and louder.

It still wasn't enough. Zinzi shadowed my thoughts until I searched the crowd for her, but she'd never be here or see me like this. *Pity.* A growing chunk of my heart needed to show her the darkest parts of my kink-fucked soul, but I couldn't scare her away like that. I couldn't lose her.

Wouldn't lose her.

She seared herself soul deep in me, and there was no way my unhealthy little obsession could let her go. I'd fallen well out of the realm of lust and into love with my friendly Friday night booty call, and she wasn't having a bar of it.

To the point she once threw a textbook my way in the middle of campus and told me she hated me just to prove to herself that she could.

But Zin forgot that hate sex is the best.

Fuck, I could almost taste her brand of bliss on my lips, mingling with the sweat and a trickle of blood that dripped into my mouth as I roared my victory for the crowd's approval.

Then I saw it and my breath hitched. Well, her. Dressed in tight, black leather pants and a red bustier that practically spilled her breasts over the top. Her long, glossy raven hair tumbled over her shoulders.

Zinzi's in the crowd.

Watching me.

But she couldn't be. She didn't know I fought, and despite my craving to grant her access to my twisted heart I wasn't about to divulge my innermost and highly illegal activities to the rumor mill of the marketing student body on campus. No one knew how to spin shit better than that group. Coming from a law major, that was saying a lot.

I searched the crowd for her again, but Zinzi's apparition had disappeared. My heart pounded, but I couldn't spot a single glossy black curl or the red bustier anywhere. I shook my head, bringing myself back to the present where Jericho unlocked the cage and let me out.

The saggy bastard counted off a thick wad of bloodstained bills and stuffed them into my hand while I scanned the crowd. When he was done I walked past him without a word and over to where I left my change of clothes earlier.

We both knew I'd be back the next week.

For now...I got to go home and torture myself with the obsessive little image of a girl who hated me enough to fuck me like she cared.

CHAPTER THREE

ZINZI

I ran through my schedule in my head as I left my last class for the afternoon. My eleven a.m. coffee didn't make it through the afternoon and three p.m.itis hit me hard. I had a two hour gap to fill with options to either head back to my room and bore myself silly before my six o'clock class—*who sets those?*—aim for the bar, which was never a good choice in the afternoon, at least for me, or hit the library.

My lecturer gave me a grand total of three new assignments to complete by the end of the month, so that last was a no-brainer.

Library it is.

I took the next branching path that led past the

common where a colorful array of college students lounged on the manicured lawn, studying, chatting...flirting.

My jeans seemed too tight as I walked. The air wasn't muggy but I struggled past the amorous students who filled every inch of the grassed space. My hand clamped tight on my laptop strap as I prayed I didn't see anyone I knew. However social I might be in marketing class, I certainly didn't maintain many friendships outside my lectures apart from my roommate and a couple of dormmates, and let's be honest—those were by necessity.

Marketing students and business majors were meant to be one of the party units on campus, but my social life was the equivalent to the history department—dry with a little eruption every now and then. Those came in the form of Dex's hot-blooded male body once a week to keep any untimely urges in check.

My one regular weekly social date with Dex made him the perfect fuck buddy of choice. He took my mind off everything that left me jittery with the sort of anxiety that would cripple most of the population, and the man could flirt like he was born to the skillset.

And fuck like it, too.

Plus, a once-a-week fuck date with him meant that I didn't need to pretend to like him hanging off me every other day through the week and be all mundane like everyone else. We filled a need for each other, appreciated each other's bodies, and got the hell out of each other's way until the next Friday rocked around.

Rinse, repeat.

A message I kept telling my body, my heart and my brain whenever they decided he wanted more out of our hot blooded male of choice. Because that couldn't be. Dex would break more than hearts if I let him, and I knew firsthand what that felt like, along with a few other things, like stitches.

Never. Again.

Not ever.

My vow against campus players held strong for my last few years at Rippton U. I could hold out a little longer until I graduated.

No matter how many times my roommate herded me to frat parties on the weekends, they just weren't my style. Being in a room full of drunken people in various states of nudity and supposedly easy bantering freaked me out on a deep level. Dancing didn't favor the uncoordinated, either. Maybe PTFBHBD—post traumatic frat boy heartbreak disorder was a real thing. I snorted and earned myself more than one sideways glance as I skulked around the commons.

Nope. I could handle all that with one person, and one person only.

This girl was purely unsociable, preferring my stats to real people most of the time. I liked measurable data, something quantifiable, the sort I could trust.

Fuck me, I'm a bore. Nerd me up, baby.

I strode past the lacrosse team who surrounded a pair of girls. One laughed, twirling her bleached locks around a red-taloned finger, while the other stood frozen and looked utterly petrified. The boys picked up on her fear and upped their ribald comments that echoed across the open area.

I shook my head. *Damn jocks.*

Another reason I didn't socialize. The Allstars—read the lacrosse kings and the ice hockey team who lived in the Kingsman frat house on campus, or at least three varsity teams full of self-appointed heroes—took top ranking in Rippton's social pecking order.

Someone like me sat at the bottom of that ladder, and I was happy to stay right there.

Unnoticed, and unseen.

A wolf whistle filled the air behind me. I looked

around cautiously to see who might have earned the attention. Just because I didn't socialize didn't mean that I wasn't a curious kitten, after all. Marketing student, you know.

My search yielded nothing except for the attention of a few jocks who eyed me with various states of sneers. I picked up my pace, keen to reach the cool interior of the library and get the hell away from everyone else. Another whistle filled the commons. I hugged my laptop bag tighter.

Please don't be for me.

But I was a nobody by my own design, so that was unlikely to happen. Especially dressed in my biker boots and jeans like I wore every day, paired with a cute little cropped, white knit cardigan over the top. I left my hair out and as usual, it was a mass of messy curls that stuck to everything, including me.

Pushing loose strands back that clung to my face, I ran my fingers through my hair and made it another three steps before someone grabbed my arm. I shrieked, one hand raised in a not-quite defensive measure, wheeling about to land face-to-face with Dex.

Razored dark brown hair hung rakishly across one eye while the rest was cut short. His lopsided smile warmed me the way it shouldn't since the first day we met at the campus bar, and he wore his typical uniform of a black button down cotton shirt, black jeans and black Converse.

The law department never looked so sexy.

I still hated him.

Repeating that mantra over and over in my head to make sure it stuck while my heart jittered away in my chest, I resumed my pace after glaring at him.

"Dex."

"Hey." He fell into step beside me.

"Is this your new scare tactic? Frighten me, so you can come over early?" I snapped.

Or see if you can call my bluff?

A power play seemed his type of thing. Push and push and push and see what happened. See what broke. But Dex wouldn't like the outcome of calling my bluff because he wasn't the sort of guy who liked to lose. Being the star of the law department told its own story.

Funny thing about not liking to lose—because neither did I.

I sneaked a sideways look at him. The bruising might've faded, but the slight yellow patch around his eye was nothing new. At least, not to me. He didn't seem to realize that I could catalog every cut and scar, every new decoration added to his taut body each week. I clocked when he got new ink, let him talk about it if he wanted. Didn't press if he didn't. Not my business, though I enjoyed listening to his reasoning if he chose to share.

Going to watch him fight—on my own, no less— had been a huge risk but oh boy, had it paid off. I thought he might have seen me in the crowd on Saturday night, the night after I last kicked him out of my room. I mean, it's not like I had a social life to schedule, and I didn't wear a white tee with my boobs busting out the bottom, or gold lamé like the over-primped ring bunnies overpopulating the edge of the cage that he fought in. They all seemed to congregate around the wired shut door, hoping for a quick fuck with a victorious fighter minutes after they left the ring.

No one touched the loser, assuming he could leave under his own steam and wasn't dragged out by a bunch of muscle on hand and planted in a corner to recover.

No, being a ring side bunny held no appeal to me, not even for Dex whose sex appeal skyrocketed as he shook the cage and roared back at the crowd who screamed his name, delirious for his attention.

I didn't have to do that, because our hate/fuck

relationship ensured he returned to my bed once a week to equalize our hormones and provided mind bending orgasms in both directions.

Nor did he give the gold lame crowd a second glance as he took the blood stained money stuffed into his fist and strode away.

No matter how I felt about him at any other point in time, Dex Breaker was *mine*.

Every one of the women clustered at the edge of the cage mooned over his retreating back. I couldn't have been more pleased at his lack of attention to them as I slipped away before he busted me perving on his bloodied, bruised and sweaty ass like every other female there.

After all, I already knew what he looked like naked and what he could do with the tools creation gifted to him. I'd wanted to see what was marking him up. I knew, really, because there were enough whispers in the Rippton rumor mill about illegal Saturday night fights for cash and favors. Even without many friends I was privy to those. But what I saw in him went well beyond a simple punch up.

Dex Breaker was a god in that cage. Maybe graduating up from a little 'g' to something bigger for the one hundred and eighty seconds the door was wired shut. Because it never—not once in the eight fights I witnessed—took him longer than that to leave his opponent unconscious and bleeding on the stained cement floor.

Dex Breaker was brutal and sexy as all get out.

The muscly as all hell object of my obsession bumped his hip against mine, bringing me back to the present where we walked across campus in daylight, not a fighting cage, no dim lights or a screaming crowd to be seen. His name faded from my mind as he stared at me, his humor slipping away in lieu of something more pensive behind the shadows shifting behind his eyes.

"Me, frighten you? Nah, too easy. Anyway, I thought I could walk a pretty girl to class."

I snorted. "Might want to check your schedule, Einstein. Mine are done for a few hours. I'm headed to the library."

He thought I was pretty? I mean, I knew that, too. He'd have to. He'd been fucking me for the better part of two and a half years.

"Better yet. Now I've got someone to pass the hours with before my night classes. Nap time?" Dex waggled his eyebrows as he loped along beside me, standing a good foot taller above my five feet and six inches—with my boots on.

"You don't nap with someone who doesn't like you," I pointed out.

His height certainly made him easy to pick out in a crowd. But it was time to put a pin in this social thing he seemed to think we had going.

"I'm wounded." He faked taking an arrow to his chest—a very defined chest where I knew the contours intimately. The corners of his lips curled up in a sinful smile. "You like the number of times you come on my cock." His gaze slid sideways, eye fucking me in public without reservation.

Yup, that was Dex Breaker for you.

"Shh," I hissed, grabbing his elbow and hauling him away from the edge of the crowd who would never have heard him anyway, but my anxiety deluged me in a massive overdose.

"What?" He straightened, the picture of innocence and all that bullshit that never matched up with the picture he presented, and he damn well knew it. "I'm just walking with the girl I love—"

"Stop. It." My face flamed at his fake as fuck declaration.

"—to fuck," he added with a wicked gleam in his eyes. "Just walking across campus. With a pretty girl. For a library based nap between classes. Is that so wrong?"

"Your negotiation skills astound me." I rolled my eyes and realized I still clung to his arm. Detaching my fingers in a hurry I shook them out like I could remove the shape and warmth of him from my hands. *Fail.* "Okay. No, you're not. Walking. With me. Or napping. Anywhere." I slowed my pace and gulped air, praying for brain function to resume. This *always* happened with him around. Always. Which added to my reserve of hate I kept just for him. "I've got assignments to work on."

I strangled my laptop strap as the catcalls came again. Without conscious thought I slid a little closer to Dex, unashamedly using him as a shield between me and the rest of the world. He glanced down at me, surprise lighting in his eyes. A small smile, different from the one of a moment before, curved his lips. Damnit, either one was too sexy for daylight hours.

And now I was thinking about those lips on my pussy, his lips doing things no lips and tongue should be able to do while I scratched my fingers through his hair and—

"I can study, you know." He threw a range of insults and the bird over his shoulder at the Allstars, flipping the lacrosse team off, seemingly missing my beetroot face that felt like it might burn my skin off at a moment's notice.

"Studying? You? The golden boy who reads something once and remembers *all*?" I made a grand show of his abilities, heedless of the audience behind us.

My snark was back on.

Good.

It always came out to play with Dex. He could be the sweetest, kindest man I'd come across, which was the only reason I trusted him in my bed. His smarts outclassed everyone else I knew, and he never bothered to hide it. Reason number two why he got to have a weekly encore session. And that confidence was the other reason I kept up our weekly get together.

It was also the reason I drew a line between fucking and hating and dating. I'd been hurt enough times that I couldn't let my heart go out like that again. Dex had more than enough nous to twist my heart *and* my head around then shatter both with the slightest blow.

Points to his favor that he didn't take home any of the ring bunnies even though we'd never pledged exclusivity to each other.

Yup, I still hated him.

He still stared over my head.

I elbowed him, drawing his attention back to me. *That was a mistake.* I cleared my throat. "Don't antagonize them. They're bad enough."

Dex rubbed a scarred hand over his jaw. "They need to be taken down a rung."

My gaze shot up in an alarm, catching and holding his. "Don't get yourself into any trouble. I know you're bored as batshit with your coursework, but come on. Taking on a full team? As if you could do that."

No matter his skill level at whatever fighting game he played, if he touched one of the teams, he'd end up bleeding out on the ground in some remote location. The fight club rumors weren't the only active ones on campus.

"Is that what you think?" He raised an eyebrow, a cocky little smirk decorating his stunning face.

That's not playing fair.

"Even you aren't that fucking stupid." Ignoring my twitching ovaries, I closed my eyes and kept walking for a few steps. My footfalls echoed on alone. I opened my eyes and pivoted. Dex had stopped a few paces behind me. "What's wrong?"

"This. Us." His intense stare pierced me as he prowled forward, closing the distance between us.

My hands hit his chest right over his heart, the ridges of muscle evident beneath the fine black cotton button down shirt he wore. Always he dressed in black on black. It suited him far too well. Something else I was certain he was aware of. I took a full step backward in a hasty retreat before he stopped, looming over me. A predatory gleam full of sin and seduction lit his hooded gaze.

"What the hell are you doing?" I whispered. "We don't fuck around during the week."

We don't do anything during the week. And sure as fuck never in front of anyone else.

My rules, my game. That's how we played.

Until it looked like he wanted to change the rules.

Dex pinned me with a hard stare, the dark fire in his eyes present after his fight burning there now. "You don't have a clue what I'm capable of," he groused.

Before I could make a choice to move, his calloused, scarred hands closed around my hips, jerking me into him. His hard body crushed to mine, his mouth searing a path against my lips that ignited desire in me on command. Pleasure unfurled low in my belly as he kissed me like a starved man intent on his final meal. The insults, the banter—that was just how we played. But the moment his mouth touched mine, my defenses scattered. My hatred dissolved at the intimate contact and I sank into his touch, melting against him.

It was like he had trained my body to respond to his whim. And I hated that too, but I couldn't bring myself to do anything about him right now. Not with the way he held me to him—possessive, dangerous. Capable of everything he promised.

And I wanted more of him.

Shots of arousal trickled up my thighs, leaving me a hot, wet mess in the middle of the commons. As though reading my mind, Dex slid hand down my lower back and over the curve of my ass, pulling me into his erection that pressed through his jeans against my stomach.

"We don't do this, Dex," I panted into his mouth, trying to ignore the chatter around us.

They don't care. We're just another couple.

But while I sat low on the social ladder, Dex was the polar opposite—adored, emulated. Untouchable. He was never seen with anyone, not even at parties.

...Until right now.

I wanted to snap at him, call him for everything under the sun for destroying the camouflage I spent years putting into action to not be seen. Instead, I clung to his shirt and played with the buttons like I might flick each one open right there and spread my hands across the familiar inked skin canvas inside.

The world shrank to just us then expanded, my awareness of others potentially watching our public display unsettling me until I wanted to hide in his arms—and I refused to do that.

"I want more of you," he grated the words against my lips, barely letting me up for air as I swallowed his.

My brow furrowed as I tried to follow his train of thought, too heady with his kisses to think straight. "What do you mean? Do you want a Wednesday night, too?"

He had to mean midweek. It couldn't be any earlier, or his bruises and cuts would be right there on display, and he wouldn't be able to deny fighting any longer.

He wouldn't be able to lie to me, still.

I'd never seen anything as sexy or arousing as watching Dex in that cage, destroying the often much older and hardened fighters he took on. I watched him tear through each man who opposed him. He dropped them all and still had enough energy to rile the crowd into a frenzy afterward.

I'd gone home to a little frenzy of my own.

Dex breathed hard against my mouth until we were sharing the same breath. "This, us. I need to see you more than once a week. I want to take you out for dinner. Tonight. And next week. Cook breakfast for you in the morning." He pressed kisses along my jaw, nipped at the corner of my mouth until I moaned softly for him.

This has to stop.

You hate him, remember?

But those lines blurred right now, and I wasn't sure where I stood under his new terms. Terms that meant he'd treat me like a princess, a possession.

Terms I hadn't agreed to, not now or ever.

"*No.*" I found my strength and pushed him away, holding him at arm's length, though it was nowhere near far enough. "We don't do that, Dex."

His eyes narrowed as I detached myself from his body with effort. "You mean *you* don't do that." His glance was scathing as he stepped into me, not giving me any chance of reprieve as he stole my ability to breathe all over again. "You're too damn scared of falling for someone, even when they're right in front of you."

"What, you?" I lashed back. *I can't do this. Not now, not ever. Not again.* Heedless of the eyes that might or might not be watching us fight in the middle of campus in the middle of the afternoon I stared up at him defiantly, clinging to the thin measure of control between us that hadn't frayed yet. "I've got shit to do."

With that poor parting shot I pushed him away again. This time, he let me. Some small but critical part of my heart wished he hadn't.

Dex's lips were set in a hard, white line, his sexy as fuck features frozen. But it was the disappointment in his eyes that forced me to place one foot before the next in a green mile walk that lasted an eternity. Because that disappointment meant we could go back to hating each other, fucking with no feelings attached.

I couldn't have it any other way.

But despite the coldness I used as armor between me and the searing heat of his gaze at my back, the walk to the library never felt so long.

Or so lonely.

CHAPTER FOUR

DEX

Zinzi's juices flooded my mouth as I lashed her clit with my tongue to the soundtrack of her screams. Her muted screams, anyway, the ones she hid behind her fist as she came, over again. Her toned thighs trembled against my shoulders where I pressed her legs open. I fisted my cock once, pushing back my own need as she creamed on my tongue.

When her arched back settled to the mattress I pulled my hand away from her stomach and pressed two fingers inside her pussy just to feel her clamp down on me before her next climax hit.

"Oh, fuck," she gasped, riding out the waves of pleasure that smashed her like a king tide. "I need you inside me."

I gritted my teeth. "And if I said no to fucking you tonight?" I found her dark eyes, held them through the next wave of bliss as confusion set in. Pushed my fingers deeper and held her hostage there on the edge of perfection. "Just kept the orgasms coming and coming...like you," I whispered as she crashed again.

"I—" Zin's eyes fluttered shut. Her hands clenched on my shoulders and slipped to the mattress, her fingers fluttering.

I smiled, and slid my fingers out of her pussy, cleaning up the mess on her thighs before I made her ache again.

And again.

Her screams were my soundtrack and we were far from done on this playlist.

I didn't fuck Zinzi on Friday night, and I left with the worst case of self-inflicted blue balls I'd ever given myself, but I set out to prove a point.

We were good for each other in so many ways. I could make her feel good and it didn't have to be with my cock buried inside her sweet, tight walls that made her feel that way, even if sex of some variety was involved.

And when I left her room, after making sure she passed out, delirious but not dehydrated—I wasn't that sort of asshole—I made sure I sneaked in a good hour of cuddles while she drooled on my chest and even purred a little.

Not that Zin remembered a damn thing. Because I made sure of that, too.

The hours I worked her body hard, leaving her trembling again and again, proved another point.

No one else can give you what I can.

You're safe in my arms, Zin. Let go.

She already knew that; it's why we had a standing once a week arrangement. But it didn't hurt to remind her while I was rocking my other agenda home in a not so delicate way. Because I knew my little hellcat would be roused as fuck when she realized she didn't get cock as advertised come tomorrow.

And I wanted to be ready for her when she came to find me on that front.

Not that I objected to extra time between the sheets—or in any other room at her place or mine midweek, that being the overall goal—but she wouldn't be getting cock off me that easily just because she was horny.

If she got horny after what I just did to her, assuming I got it right. From the way she purred and sighed as I crept out of her dorm room after pressing a tender kiss to her temple, passing her roommate, Margot, in the hallway who made eyes at me as we crossed paths and pretended each other didn't exist, I didn't think I missed the mark.

Okay, so maybe I had a secondary goal: make Zinzi Jones fall head over heels for me the way I'd already tumbled for her.

Long, long ago.

This was the girl I'd do anything for, and I knew it. Now, I needed to make sure she felt the same way about me. If that meant providing her with an unlimited source of orgasms in a campaign to redefine our Friday night fuck fests and their purpose, then so be it.

I had a midweek game plan too, but that could wait for phase two. Or maybe three. I wanted to see how she reacted to this part of the plan first.

Throwing my varsity jacket over my shoulders that just fit, I shoved my hands into my pockets and tucked my chin against the night's bitter chill, hightailing it across campus to my own room. Why we couldn't be a simple building apart, I had no idea. It was like Rippton was determined to make my walk of shame as cold and as long as possible in the worst months of the year.

Muttering obscenities to myself and flexing my fingers in a bid to regain feeling to my fingertips, I pushed my door open and came face to face with three men who did not belong in my room whatsoever.

Beau Bennett rested his overpriced Kingsman frat worthy ass against the edge of my sofa. His lip curled up like he wanted to be anywhere else. I'd clocked his attention on my girl earlier in the week when I caught up with Zin crossing the common and kissed the shit out of her to prove another point—apparently I was all sharp edges this month.

The billionaire dark horse prince of Rippton U and head of the Kingman frat house as well as captain of the lacrosse team, I could deal with. The other two—

They were a different matter.

Two blond twins, so close in looks they were beyond identical, stood in my shared, L-shaped kitchenette. One flipped his phone in his hands, while his brother toyed with my knife block.

A visit from Key and Kash Laurent was never a good omen.

I shut the door gently and prayed Nelson wasn't at home. "Falcon's out with his father at some beach on the coast. He should be back next week," I added softly as I hung my jacket on the hook behind the door. Every movement I made, I kept casual, my tone remaining relaxed and light.

Turning my back to these three predators felt like the grossest neglect, but then, no amount of watching would keep me alive if the twins decided to wade into that arena. It wouldn't matter how many scratches there were beneath my name on the post if the knives came out of the block because these boys didn't play nice, and I already fought dirty.

I'd still lose.

And Beau Bennett would dance in my blood before he left my room. That was the sort of twisted fucker he was. Falcon Gianio wasn't the only mafia prince at Rippton U, though he and Beau traditionally gave each other a wide berth—until right now.

The corners of Beau's mouth flickered up. "We aren't here for Falcon."

Double fuck. I really hoped Nelson wasn't at home.

His lordship chose that moment to waltz right

through the too narrow hallway connecting our bedrooms wearing nothing but a towel and a white and pink spotted bowtie—don't ask. I stopped over a year ago.

Beau jerked his head once. The twins moved with the sort of grace and synchronicity that would make a ballerina turn all the shades of Kermit.

Two blond heads, so white they were almost pigmentless, glided toward my roommate like they were ghostly shadows. The barest shout left my throat before a hand closed on mine and I had my own fight to deal with.

I shoved Beau's chin back, losing sight of Nelson instantly, but determined to do some sort of damage to his spine as he seemed intent on flattening my esophagus. None of that mattered as I twisted my head in time to see the twins close in on my utterly naive and unaware roommate who went down like a sack of flour the moment they ran right over him.

Nelson's name died a short and abrupt death on my lips as I wheezed and finally managed to roll Beau beneath me. My fist slammed into the carpet in the place where his head had been a second before the hard barrel of a gun pressed to my midsection.

"I'm sure you're attached to whatever is right

here, so I'd stop, now." Beau spoke slow, clear and fucking loud.

No one could miss the threat in that sentence.

I leaned back in my straddle over him, my hands raised, but I didn't look at the man who could end my life with one feathered finger on his trigger. If he wanted to do that, I'd be dead already. My gaze locked onto the twins who dragged a dazed and naked—apart from the bow tie, of course—Nelson into the middle of the living area.

"What the fuck did he do to you?" I addressed Beau without taking my eyes off the twins.

Whatever they did to Nelson, I'd revisit on them tenfold. I made the overprotective promise in an instant. Nelson might be annoying, he might be frustrating, but at the end of the day he was just a weird kid who never quite fit in. And he wasn't an asshole. I could have worse for a housemate.

"Actually, it's not him we're here for. It's you." Beau hauled his ass out from beneath my bulk, and pocketed the gun. He nodded. Nelson's fragile, pasty form slumped in the middle of the room.

"What did I do?" I looked at him for the first time, pleased to clock the bruising that bloomed around his throat.

"You won," he said simply. "I need you to lose."

It took me less than half a minute to catch on, and I groaned. "Fucking betting ring. And you think I'll do what you want?" I raised both eyebrows and folded my arms.

Beau shrugged and a twin—I couldn't tell them apart—extracted a knife, leaning over Nelson's form.

I gritted my teeth. *Asshole.* "How often do I need to lose?"

"Let's start with tomorrow night. How about you throw the last fight?" His eyes glittered at me. "A kick to the ribs should do it. And as an added incentive, if you don't, it won't be the little lordling here who ends up with a new scar. It'll be the pretty girl with the dark hair."

Zin.

I opened my mouth to call the son of a bitch for every name he earned just for thinking of her, but he put a finger to his lips.

"Shhh. I won't tell if you won't. Now, let's get a schedule together, shall we?"

I ground my teeth at the presumptuous shit's attitude knowing he could do anything he wanted while he held Zin's safety over my head.

On the floor, Nelson began to moan as the twins cut into him anyway.

CHAPTER FIVE

ZINZI

I kept my head down and tried to pretend the world didn't exist. Not an easy job when the object of my unaffection kept staring at me from the library in the row three across from mine at half an hour before the building closed for the night. A Wednesday night, when we weren't supposed to be near each other anyway.

As per usual, Dex decided to play by his own rules, not mine. Just like he did last Friday night. Because it wasn't until a solid hour until after he left that I realized we hadn't had sex.

Let me tell you straight: Zinzi was not okay.

I mean, that was the whole point of our deal,

right? He came around. We played, we teased the shit out of each other. We drove each other insane. Sometimes we tried new sexual stuff we hadn't before because even though we were both rough as hell together, Friday night with Dex was a safe—if orgasmic—space. We came, we fucked and he left.

End of story.

Only this time, he turned up, I came—a *lot*—and then he left.

With me satisfied. And also unsatisfied. Because I wasn't aching and I wasn't burning.

Because even after all the orgasms he could possibly provide for me between the hours of nine p.m. and midnight on a Friday night, I still felt empty.

He didn't come either. My blissful, Dex-induced haze told me that much, too. He held off for me, and I had no idea what to make of that. None of it was part of our deal.

Play, fuck, come. Leave.

Repeat exactly one week later.

We had been onto this good thing for just over two years and now...

Dex Breaker changed the rules we played by. My damn rules, and I wasn't happy with that. Not one bit.

To top it off, he had spent the last two hours, I had counted both, every single minute that passed, and gotten very little work done in the interim, while he watched me with love lorn eyes like I was the object he focused on.

During the wrong day of the week.

And I was done.

I pushed back my handwritten assignment—I was a pen and paper draft girl—and shoved my chair across the tiled flooring at the same time as he rose. I froze in place. Dex grinned as he made his way across to my table, resting his perfectly formed ass against the corner, still giving me enough room to breathe, the courteous asshole.

"Are we going?" He walked his fingers across the table top, over my mostly blank page—also courtesy of him—and up my bare arm. Those same rough, inked fingers slipped under the strap of my tank top and tugged lightly.

My body flushed on demand. I hated the reaction he had pre-programmed into me.

"I still have work to do—"

The library ten minute warning bell for closing time echoed through our floor, the lights flickering twice just to rub the point in.

Okay, so I don't have thirty minutes left, after all.

"You were saying?" The grin never left his face.

"You knew what time it was," I grumbled, stacking my books together and shoved them into my postie satchel next to my laptop that he held open for me.

Also, courteous.

"What are you, going for extra brownie points this week? It doesn't count if it doesn't go in," I said somewhat pointedly as one page slithered to the floor and ended up beneath the desk I'd been working at.

Dex snorted, bending way too lithely to collect the runaway paper. "Why does this have my name doodled all over it and is decorated with little stabby knives?" he asked idly, onyx eyes glinting as he passed my page up to me from a kneeling position.

One hand rested on the seat I'd been working on, the other, once free of the rogue paper, slid up my thigh to rest just below my hip.

I swallowed. "I was feeling particularly violent."

"And now?"

"I could employ a different weapon." I planted my boot between his legs and lifted the toe just enough to graze his balls through his black jeans.

Dex bared his teeth in a feral smile. "I knew I

loved you for a reason, Zin. You've always got my best interests at heart." He stayed in that position for a moment longer after dropping a little love bomb of his own while I glared at him.

"Keep testing me, big boy. You already screwed up my study session." I pushed the words out through clenched teeth and by some grace I didn't know I possessed, managed not to remove his ability to bear children. I mean, being annoying didn't get him there—quite—but it was a close thing.

"Just keeping an eye on my girl."

I opened my mouth to object that I was not in fact his girl, or anything else, and that the agreement we had was limited to one night a week alone, when he rose fluidly to tower over me, planting his hands on either side of the desk. One braced behind me. Dex's breath brushed my lips, and that was the breath I breathed in when mine evicted from between startled lips.

"You—"

"Ready to go?"

His eye hit glitterball territory, the dangerous sort, as he drew back just far enough to let me inhale untainted air.

"I would have been done an hour or more ago," I

snapped, slinging my bag across my chest and stepping around him.

Only the strap never hit my chest. I grabbed for it, and spun on my heel to find Dex adjusting my satchel over his own chest. He patted the bag at his side as I gaped at him.

"Like I said, ready to go? I'll walk you back."

"I really don't need it." I'd started this conversation with snark and I saw no reason to stop now.

Dex's turn on sweetness confused the hell out of me. We'd never been these people—or him this person—who waited for me after my silent, solo study sessions into the night avoiding my roommate and her random hookups, the campus social scene, or any sort of human connection at all. And now, he had a hostage.

I eyed my bag and twitched my nose. "You know I'm gonna need that back."

"As soon as we reach your dorm. After you." He waved me out of the stacks, his heavy, regular footfalls on the worn tiles an odd comfort at my back.

My stomach flopped over at the concept. Damnit, I liked the fact that he was there way too much.

"You know, you don't have to do this," I started as the automatic doors to the library's broad front opened. I waved to the librarian on duty over my shoulder as I started down the steps. One of the fourth year students. I couldn't remember her name.

"Bye, Dex," she called far too brightly for this time of night.

"Bye, Elizabeth," he tossed back. I could *hear* the smile in his voice, for feck's sake.

"You don't have to be so indecently happy. I mean, does she go by Liz or Lizzy when you screw her midweek? Is that what you gave up to haunt my table tonight?" I groused, unable to stop the reflux burning my throat.

Yup, that's what we were going with. Reflex.

Dex cast me an amused sideways glance as he caught up with me. "I don't have a clue. Her name tag read Elizabeth, so that's what I called her." He shrugged.

"Yeah, you're a regular Darcy."

"Nah. I don't have the hair to pull that off."

I shortened my stride, surprised he caught the reference and decided to throw an extra test out, because my personal asshole factor was high tonight, and I was low on caffeine. "Which version?"

Dex's head tipped to one side. "I'm partial to MacFayden. But also, Colin Firth did it better. Preference?"

"Nineteen ninety-five."

"Ah, we agree."

I nodded, then caught myself and scowled. "Don't rig your answers to suit me."

"I would never." Dex held out both hands in defense.

"And protect my laptop." The hands went back to my bag. I smiled. "Good boy."

"I can be trained."

A snort left me. "Not likely. You, housebroken? Come on." I nudged his shoulder with mine, and looked up when he didn't budge. His gaze was fixed at a point over my head. I adjusted my view along the dimly lit path that forked between my dorm and his, wrapping my arms around myself. I wished I'd brought a jacket. "Distraction," I muttered.

"Yeah." Dex ran his fingers through his hair and wrapped his arm around my shoulders, tugging me toward the path that led away from my room. "Fancy a drink?"

"At this hour?" I flicked my wrist over to check my watch where I wore it facing into me. "Dex, it's—"

"Not even ten thirty," he said smoothly. "Remember how we met?"

"At the bar during orientation week?" I raised

both eyebrows. "Weren't you pissed as a parrot and I had to tow you around as your guide for the day? I watched you puke on four campus plants that have since died," I reminded him.

"One has resurrected," he proclaimed proudly, steering us in the direction of the bar.

His fingers massaged my bare shoulder. I soaked in the warmth of him and let him, pretending the flirty librarian hadn't bothered me at all.

It's just one drink.

"No, it died," I muttered, tipping my head down so my hair covered my face, and my grin.

"It's alive and well. I can show you right now," Dex protested.

"I replaced it."

"What?" He stopped and turned me to face him.

"I bought a new one. I figured we shouldn't have killed four plants in one day and I felt guilty. So I replaced one. It's all I could afford. I'm not a rich kid like some people." I bit my lip, but my grin wouldn't stay hidden, even with my hair curtain.

Dex dropped his arm and rocked back onto his heels, his face the picture of a stunned mullet. "You bought a plant and you never told me?" he blinked. "I thought for years that thing lived on."

"From the power of your acidic spew." I clapped

one hand to his chest, and he winced. I paused. "What happened to you?"

"Cracked rib," he muttered, and closed his eyes like he hadn't wanted the admission to slip out.

"How?" I raised both eyebrows, some of my humor fading.

"Beau Bennett. Fighting." He held up a hand. "Just...don't ask. I got it checked at the hospital on Saturday."

"Saturday." I counted in my head. "That's four days ago."

"Yeah."

And we don't have the sort of relationship where you could have messaged me and told me.

"Who drove you home from the hospital?" I said finally.

"I walked."

I closed my eyes, fighting back the dual wave of anger and terror that sickened me on so many fronts. *I told you so* wouldn't fix anything right now, but something else might. "Are you on painkillers?"

"Yeah, but I haven't used them."

"Good."

"Why?"

"It's my shout tonight."

~

Dex stumbled along my hallway. I couldn't tell who giggled worse—me, or him.

Distraction achieved.

I hadn't meant for either of us to get riotously drunk with my Friday night entertainment, *or* dance on the tables, but hey, not all things went to plan.

Certainly not my not when he cornered me against the doorframe to my room as I finally managed to free my keys before something along those lines happened. His hips pressed to mine, holding me in place. Not hard like he would if he was about to start something. My confused gaze met his— more discombobulated than ever when his hands cupped my cheeks and he lowered tender lips to mine.

Lips that tasted of hops from the last craft beer we shared.

"What are you doing?" I murmured, a little stunned when he drew back. His large hands still cupped my jaw, and his thumbs brushed the sides of my throat gently.

"Kissing you." Dex dipped his head before I could reply.

His lips brushed mine, then his tongue sought

entry—but in a sweet, gentle kiss that blew my mind from the sheer tenderness of his touch. He tipped my head back for better access and my body moved with him because we *knew* this man, trusted him intimately even if I'd never admit to it with anyone else.

A soft sound slipped from my lips. He answered with an approving one of his own as he delved deeper, still with that same sensuous, tender kiss that lifted me against him like I floated on air or some stronger emotion that I didn't want to admit to right now.

Oh so slowly, Dex drew back, leaving our lips grazing gently against each other in an undeniably intimate caress that would have left me shivering any other time. Only tonight, he'd stolen my ability to react. I sank into the warmth of his hands where they cupped my face. His scarred, calloused palms were a familiar strength I rested against as I struggled to pry dozy eyes open.

He came into view when I blinked languidly. The shiver that wracked me started at the base of my nape and rippled along my spine in slow motion. I trembled in his hands as he made a second approving noise low in his throat, and managed to turn the key in the lock that my hand had forgotten it held.

"Let me come in," Dex murmured in a low voice. "Let me look after you tonight, Zin."

Hell, even his voice was sexy, deep and raspy like that.

"I— What day is it?" I leaned back, swaying in his hands.

The corner of his mouth crooked up. "Does it matter?"

"It should." My brain wasn't braining. "I'm sure it's supposed to."

"It doesn't. Not anymore." He leaned in to kiss me again, pushing my door open with his boot.

"Are you home, finally? I was going to call the cavalry. And you—" Margot, my roommate, popped her head out of the doorway just as Dex maneuvered us inward. We got stuck in a strange three-way, one body headed in the opposite direction to the rest of us.

"Margot?" I twisted in Dex's arms, and he let out a snort.

"Isn't it the wrong day for the big guy to visit? I'm not vacating." Margot planted her feet firmly on the threadbare carpet that formed our threshold.

The same one that Dex crossed the last Friday

night after we didn't fuck. After all those orgasms. The night he broke my rules.

On Friday.

I turned accusing eyes to him. "It's not Friday."

Margot crowed triumphantly. "Not getting kicked out of my own room tonight, sucker!" She wandered off across to her bedroom, her job done, leaving me alone with Dex.

I slid my hand beneath the strap to my laptop satchel and tugged it over his head, ignoring my pounding heart, the way my breath refused to stay in my chest and the fact that I had to get up onto my toes to achieve my mission at all.

"Give. It. Back," I muttered, though he offered up no resistance whatsoever.

"It's yours." Dex spread his hands, leaning just inside the door jamb, and crooked a finger. "Come here."

"Nu uh." I retreated inside my room a few steps. "That's a really bad idea. Why don't you take your fighting, cracked ribs, your vendetta with the Allstars Captain—" I *told* him not to go after Beau, even if I hadn't mentioned the head of the Kingsman frat by name, "—and head on back to your mafia roommate. Isn't he home by now?"

"Yeah. Brought a pretty little thing with him."

"Good, why don't you share? I'm sure you like that." I turned away and stopped, the force on my arm holding me in place.

I looked down at his giant hand wrapped around my entire shoulder, his palm warm but not half as welcoming as his embrace had been a second before when he had kissed the hell out of me. Scars and ink decorated his knuckles. I studied each then looked over my shoulder and found his gaze.

His teeth bared. "Would you like that? Me sharing a girl with someone else? Fucking away with Falcon when you weren't there?"

I shrugged, refusing the image of the Italian sex bomb that was his housemate when it tried to pop into my mind, deflecting from the point he tried to make. "I never liked the mafia type. They spend too much time looking in the mirror for my tastes."

"You know what I meant. What if I went back to the library and found the librarian for the night? What was her name...Elizabeth?"

I hissed through my teeth and yanked my shoulder free of his hold. He let me go, opening his hand. I stumbled, forward clutching my bag. A feral sound that echoed his own ripped from my lips. I wasn't sure what hurt more—my heart, or my pride.

"Do whatever you like, Dex. I'm not your girlfriend or your keeper. We just fuck, remember? We just happen to be good at it together." Maybe if I said it enough times, I'd believe it.

His gaze hardened impossibly. "We are good together, Zin. We could be better."

"Could we?" I raised an eyebrow. "Not if you're considering hooking up with someone else."

White teeth flashed again. "That was your fucking—" He snapped the end of his sentence off, breathing hard. "I swear, Zin. There's no one else I want but you. Fuck, there hasn't been anyway *but* you since we met. Not fucking once."

My stomach dropped. Any other girl on campus might want to hear that declaration, but to me it felt like prison bars of a pretty variety. All promises simply ended up with a pedestal I had to climb with a fucking steep drop to tumble from on the other side.

Usually onto a blade of my own making. Literally.

"Maybe you should browse more. See what's out there before you make a one sided decision like that. Good night, Dex. Shut the door behind you."

I turned away so he didn't see the first tear fall.

Silence was the only thing that filled the space at my back. For a long moment, I thought he'd left.

Then those same, heavy footfalls I liked in the library following me padded closer. His fingertips grazed the line of my shoulders, beneath my hair. I thought he might say something more, then his touch disappeared, the door shut and he was gone.

No, Dex wasn't the one to see my tears fall, but Margot did.

CHAPTER SIX

DEX

Taking hits became synonymous with fucking Zin because my Friday night memories were the way I distracted myself when the easy shots came flying at my face that I had to take and take and take. I kept my hands taut at my sides as I recalled sinking balls deep in her pretty, hot little pussy and pretended the blood dripping down my face was her juices creaming on my lips.

I had to admit, she tasted better. Sounded better than Jericho screaming obscenities from the other side of the cage, too.

I flipped him off for the hell of it, delivered a roundhouse kick because I could with my eyes closed—that last because the bastard I fought had opened a cut over my eyebrow and my vision turned red in the last thirty seconds—and risked knocking the fucker out. Pity it didn't work. I would have worn Beau's wrath for that little misdemeanor.

Instead, I took a kick to the back that knocked into my healed ribs and cracked them anew. A sound like a wheezing, dying dinosaur left my lips before I could tamp it down. I slammed my fist onto the cement floor once and something else popped.

Pinkies are overrated anyway.

A boot rocked my stomach, and I spat blood onto the floor. Fuck, I was getting killed and I couldn't do a damn thing about it. I turned my head to the side, spotting Beau's ugly mug in the crowd at the back in his customary place between the twins where they flanked him like pale bodyguards.

Last time, I mouthed, and rolled sideways, facing the asshole grinning down at me. I flipped him off, too. "Heard your mother is watching. I know she's loose, but thought I'd have a go later. Show her how to give you a brother with real DNA."

The man's face purpled as his eyes bugged out comically as a vein popped somewhere around his temple. His next kick aimed for my head.

I stared at the swinging fluorescent lights inside Jericho's office from the floor and tried not to think about what the hell I was lying on. From the accumulated grit in his trailer, the man had never vacuumed in his life. The fight ring was probably cleaner. At least it got hosed down once a night.

"You gonna tell me who?"

I stared at the rusty wire the light hung from. One end that bore chew marks. "Fucking rats," I realized. "You need an exterminator or some shit."

"We aren't all fucking rich boys. Is that who's paying you to throw fights? You're fucking with my life, kid."

I turned my head. "No one is paying me to do shit." The simple motion hurt, and my stomach revolted.

Jericho pointed to the door. "If you're gonna puke, do it the fuck outside."

I shoved up and made it to the door before bile left my mouth in a projectile motion. I decorated the parking lot and heaved until my stomach flipped over a few times on a personal rollercoaster ride I didn't appreciate.

Wiping my mouth on the back of my hand I

made it back into his office and found a chair to collapse into. My ribs protested every breath as well as every cramp but my stomach didn't care about my current pain threshold.

"I'm not here for dirty money." I took the beer Jericho offered. "You gonna throw me off the fights?"

He snorted. "Not fucking likely. You bring in too much cash. But if you've got trouble, I have muscle who can help you out of it."

I stared at him, exasperated. "Then I what, owe you instead? I already have one problem. I like you. But you don't own me."

Jericho smirked. "It was worth a try."

"It really wasn't."

"You got a ride?" He frowned. "I heard your ribs go. You're not fighting for a while. I'll pay you if you can emcee for a few weeks."

"Shit, I'll do that for free. You suck."

"Little shit."

We shook on it and I walked out of his trailer, trying to flip my phone in my left hand, and fumbled the grab. My coordination sucked as badly as Jericho's fight ring callouts. From the swelling in my right hand, I'd either dislocated my pinky or broken it. Sighing, I called Falcon, but his phone rang out. I sent a message, but that bounced too.

The hell is he doing?

I flipped it again and caught it. Okay, if Falcon wasn't answering, maybe I could walk to the hospital. Again—

Which had been hell last week.

Or I could call Zin.

I flipped my phone, didn't miss the grab and dialed her number before I chickened out.

"I already saw you yesterday, Dex," she warned me when she picked up.

Her voice sounded so sweet that for a second I couldn't form words. And having her so close to the fight ring and Jericho's shithouse trailer seemed wrong, so I started walking. It didn't really matter which direction I headed in at this point.

"Hey," I muttered. "What have you got planned for tonight?"

"You're not coming over," she said immediately. "Margot's here. And she's got a...friend."

The phone shifted away from her gentle breaths that were replaced with loud moans and a few squeaks. I grinned despite the ache running through my rib cage on both sides that the beer hadn't done a damn thing to quell. *I should have hit Jericho up for a bourbon.*

"Sounds like someone is having all the fun. Are you up for a drive?" I aimed for casual.

"What the fuck did you do?" she practically shrieked at me.

Even the bouncing and moaning in the background stopped.

"Uh—" *Fucking busted.* "I could do with a lift," I hedged.

"To the hospital?" Keys jangled on her end. She yelled something, ostensibly to Margot, who yelled back in her normal voice before the moans started up again. "She's a screamer, alright?"

"Why does she leave the room for us, and you don't leave for her?" I asked, stuffing my hand in my pocket and hissed out a breath when my pinky hit the material.

"Ribs?"

"And hand. The last is my fault."

"Fuck. They're both your fault. I fucking told you not to screw around with Beau Bennett and the Allstars."

"Or the twins."

"The—" Zin said words I promised myself she had never said before tonight and never would again.

Double standards, much?

I knew she had a filthy mouth. I just only liked it when she was with me, and I was inside her. *Lie.* I liked her filthy mouth all the time.

"Where did you get such a broad vocabulary?" I asked, interested.

"I had a gay best friend when I was a kid. He has a drag act now. Damn good. In both personas he has a filthy fucking mouth."

"Why don't I know him?" I frowned.

"Because we have a standing Friday night date and not much else," she reminded me.

"And if I want more?"

"There is no more, Dex. I'm coming to get you because you screwed up."

"You're coming to get me because you care, sweetness."

"Do I? Because I can stop and you can walk," she sassed me.

But we both knew she was coming. Fuck, I hoped she was coming, because I was in for a long damn walk and I wasn't even sure what direction I picked. *Stupid ass.*

"Where are you?" she asked on cue.

"Ahhh—" I found a street corner and rattled off the nearest names, plus a few buildings as landmarks. "Don't get out of the car when you arrive," I said, keeping my voice as light as I could, despite the tightness building around my ribs and chest.

My breath puffed harder with every step but I kept my stride long and even. It wouldn't do for the twins to see my suffering, and I knew they were watching. Fuck, they weren't even here for her tonight. If they saw me struggling and were out for blood, Zin would pay for my debt.

She shouldn't be hurt because of me. Hell, Nelson already boasted a few extra scars because I couldn't keep my roommate safe.

"Nine minutes. Are you going to pass out on me?" My girl was all business.

"Nah. Keep talking. I like hearing your voice."

I kept an eye on where one of the twins parked his ass against a shadowy building further up the block. I guessed his significant other was stationed on the other side. If I timed this wrong I'd pass them on foot, and that could be catastrophic. Or I'd pass them with her—and that could be worse.

Choosing the lesser of two evils, I power walked through my pain, shoving my fear aside and prepared for a blade in my back.

It never arrived. Zin chattered nervously on the phone all the way to me, keeping me distracted nicely as well. She pulled up as the twins stalked my footsteps, changing buildings and blocks with each I passed. I never looked back, but then I didn't have to. They weren't hiding.

I never stopped, not until I slid into the car she pulled up to the curb and peeled away the moment I snapped *"Go,"* at her.

"You are filthy. He beat you good." She eyed me sideways, and reached across to yank my seat belt over me, ignoring my wince. "Shut up. You deserve it," she reproved me. "If you're going to call me, make sure I'm there when it happens next time."

"You want to see me get the shit beaten out of me?" I leaned my head back onto the passenger seat and closed my eyes, not needing an answer.

All I could think about was the night I thought I'd seen her in the crowd. Did I want her there? Fuck, yes, I did. Every damn time.

Even though it hurt like hell, I reached out with my mangled hand and grabbed hers, winding our fingers together tight, ignoring her exclamation.

After a moment, she grew quiet. Then—

"I'd kiss you, but you're covered in blood and filth."

"And puke," I added helpfully.

"Someone else's?"

"My own, Zin. Tonight fucking hurt," I admitted.

More silence. I could deal with that. She drove.

"Why?"

"Huh?" I blinked at street lights going past upside down. My stomach hated that. "Ugh."

"Why do you fight him?"

Beau. She still thought I was fighting Beau Bennett. "Ah—it's the rush. He's an ass. It's off campus." A shitty lie, maybe plausible? I had no idea.

"Bullshit. Not buying it." She stroked my hand, the not sore side.

"That feels nice."

"Good." She stopped the car. "We're here, Dex. Get out. I'll go find a parking spot."

"Oh." I found the ER sign with bleary eyes, and looked back at her. "Thanks for driving." I wanted to kiss her, but she was right. I was filthy.

She clicked her tongue and gave me a little push towards the door. "I can't stop here, Dex. Get out. I'll come find you."

I nodded and hauled my ass out the door. "Thanks, Zin."

She huffed out a breath and drove away. For the first time in hours, I smiled. At least she'd be well away from beau's psychotic tame twins here. I headed inside the hospital, and prepared for pain.

~

Zin dropped me home. She still refused to come in, but I got her as far as my door. Hell, I even claimed a kiss, though that might have been a painkiller-induced hallucination. The doc did me good, and I was dozy as fuck with whatever he managed to get me to keep down.

"Come in," I murmured, tugging at her arm with my good hand, walking backwards as Nelson opened the door when I kicked at it with my heel. "Stay with me."

"No." Zin glared at first me, then at my house-mate. "Enough favors for one night. Go deal with your new charge, nursemaid," she shot at Nelson, turning away.

I laced the fingers of my good hand through hers. Not that I could feel the other one in its cast right now. "What if I need you tonight?" I asked, lowering my voice, though Nelson wouldn't miss *anything* being right damn well there in our space, the royal little creeper.

"Then you'll have to take care of it yourself. With your other hand," she said tartly to Nelson's general hilarity. "Maybe think of that if you're going to pick a fight with the biggest bully on campus. Have you been fighting, too?" Her dark gaze snapped to my roommate.

Nelson took a step back, freeing the doorway up. I took the opportunity, retreating into my dorm room, and brought Zin with me.

"I don't have anything to do with this." Nelson raised his hands in my periphery, but couldn't stop the wince his action brought on.

A decent dose of guilt swirled in my stomach. "He's not involved." I doubled down on his declaration of innocence.

I mean, he was, but only because of me. And... cue the extra guilt. No amount of painkillers stopped that. Damnit.

Zin snorted. "Right." She tugged her hand free, and I couldn't stop her. Nothing worked properly, including my feet. "Go to bed, Dex. I'll be back to feed you in the morning. Look after him," she said softly to Nelson over my head as I found myself sitting on the floor. "And don't let him pick fights with Beau Bennett, for fuck's sake?"

Nelson laughed. "Yes, ma'am."

Zin leaned down into my field of vision and cupped my cheeks in her smooth, small hands. "Go to sleep, Dex. Rest. I'll—" She sighed. "I'll be here tomorrow."

I gave her a goofy grin. "I knew you couldn't resist me," I murmured, losing myself in her pretty eyes.

Right before I passed out on her biker boots and drooled across their scuffed surface.

CHAPTER SEVEN

ZINZI

I perched on the edge of Dex's sofa for the second week in a row, no more comfortable in his friend's space than I had been on my first day there, and pretended to smile. Nelson flicked at his bow tie and scrolled on his phone, while Falcon made out with his new girlfriend and returned the same assessing glance I'd been giving him for the last weeks.

None of us had made ground in the last fourteen days while Dex did the same thing he'd done the whole time I'd been in visiting mode.

He slept.

Finally, the silence of the room and Dex's snores, not that they weren't cute, exactly, I just had nothing to do while he snoozed with his head on my lap, ate at me.

"Okay," I said too loudly for the cramped space filled with five of us, standing up. Thankfully, the boys let me keep my boots on. Dex's head dropped back to the sofa, his snores continuing unhindered. "I don't think I can do much more here." My fingers twitched at my sides. I held them still with effort.

"Your company helps." Nelson offered me a small smile, toying with his bowtie and his phone at once.

That was quite a skill considering that the only other garment he wore was a towel that didn't quite disguise the long, pink scar that crept up from his midsection. There was a story in that, and I wanted to pry, but kept my mouth shut.

Falcon withdrew from kissing his girlfriend who seemed at least as shy as me and hid in his shoulder. The mafia prince, from all accounts, wasn't. He studied me baldly, his brand of silence both confident and unnerving.

"I don't really think I'm doing anything." I gestured to the sleeping Dex, who cuddled into the side of the couch.

"He doesn't sleep when you're not here," Nelson added softly, pausing in his bowtie torture.

"And he drinks all my whiskey." Falcon grimaced, breaking his silence to speak up for the first time in a day.

But the death knell came from the man I'd left snoozing on the sofa.

"Stay." Dex cracked one eye open and held out his injured hand which was, in fact, broken.

Everything with him was on a six to eight week repair schedule, minimum, and we were two weeks in. Nelson typed up his assignments as Dex dictated off the top of his head, both working at a speed that blew me away. Falcon knocked around business negotiations and tactics that taught everyone in the room more than we ever needed to know about legal loopholes. That, at least, seemed to keep Dex's mind active and stopped him from being self-destructive.

And me...

I got to play nursemaid. What I had accused Nelson of being back on that first day when I brought Dex home from the hospital all filthy and bandaged up. Which meant I was the only one in the room who was kind of useless.

"I'm not really sure why I'm here," I whispered helplessly, letting Dex take my hand.

He switched it out for his good one when his bandaged hand grew clumsy. "You're here because I need you." He drew me back to the sofa, wrapping a log-like arm around my waist.

Warmth from him sank into me, removing some of my discomfort. My period had hit yesterday and the heat of his touch eased some of the pain that assaulted my lower back like I'd been stabbed. I refused to acknowledge the other cramps, preferring to pretend they didn't exist.

I sat reluctantly, locked in a flesh and material cage of my own making. On the first day I'd refused flat out to let Dex draw me into his bedroom, knowing that we'd just end up tangled in each other's arms. That door had remained off limits since. And though screwing around seemed like our regular fun activity, it wouldn't help his ribs or his hand to heal—or my heart. Because that's who we were. We weren't this coupledom pigeon pair who he tried to meld us into.

No matter how much it hurt my heart to see him struggle with both the pain and the heartache or whatever ate him inside. Because we all sure as fuck knew that nothing laid out Dex Breaker by choice.

Not even cracked ribs and a fractured finger.

"Stay, Zin," he murmured again, stroking the back of my hand with his thumb.

I noted the deep circles under his eyes, the redness at the edges as he looked up at me beseechingly. Nelson nodded his encouragement when I glanced his way. Predictably, Falcon said nothing.

Letting out a sigh, I slid beneath Dex's raised head, and planted my ass. "I've got two hours til class. *If* you let me work here, okay?' I muttered, extracting my laptop from my bag. "Can I plug in somewhere?" I swung the end of my charge cable in a slow circle.

Nelson's face lit up, and the tension in the room broke. Even Falcon's slow growing smile took on an approving glow as he went back to making out with Bella.

"Feeling like a fifth wheel, anyone?" muttered Nelson.

I giggled, and clamped my hand over my mouth at the sound that shattered the silence in the room.

The Lord of Nothingness sent me a knowing look. "It's okay to be human and feel, Zin. We don't all have to lock our hearts away."

I raised an eyebrow. "Maybe you should go for Casanova of the Week. isn't Opal doing a stack of those for Valentine's Day this year at the campus paper?" I yawned into the back of my hand.

He shrugged. "Something like that. But who wants a displaced lord with no land, a title and some spare change?" he said lightly.

"If you consider a billion plus in the bank to be *spare change*," Falcon snorted.

"A bil—" I gaped at the Lord of Apparently Freaking Everything who crouched before me on his knees like any average pleb, plugging in my laptop charger. "Why aren't you in the Kingsman frat, and why aren't you being eccentric and getting laid?" I blurted.

Falcon laughed, long and loud. Bella, giggled into his chest.

Nelson perched on the arm of the sofa and patted my head sweetly and pointed to his bow tie. "Eccentric. And because the Kingsman frat is full of assholes. I like pussy, darling. And money isn't everything."

"Says the man with a happy nine figures in his bank account," Dex mumbled into my thigh.

I nodded, absently swiping at a collection of saliva pooling at the corner of his mouth. "My household can't make it to ten thousand," I informed Nelson. "You've outclassed us all, Lord of Bow Ties."

He grinned, flicking said bowtie in a strangling

motion that apparently still let him breathe. "That's a good title."

I grinned, and suddenly, I didn't feel as uncomfortable as I had when I walked in on my fourteenth day of nurse maiding Dex, stuffed between his mafia prince and billionaire Lordling roommates.

"Group project. What could be more fun." Nelson plopped into the seat beside me in my third year marketing class and twirled his bowtie.

I stared at him. "I didn't realize you were in this class." A class I'd been taking for the better part of a month, and I hadn't seen him in a single session.

Not once.

"I wasn't. Watching you talk about marketing and...things...encouraged my love of the art." Nelson mixed his metaphors, probably threw in an acronym while I wasn't paying attention, and waved his fingers in a completely lord-like motion I *thought* was meant to convey the magic of...something.

I snorted. "You're also full of shit."

Apparently billionaire lordlings could do what they liked on campus, all his previous declarations to the contrary.

"That I am."

"So, why are you really here?" I peeked at the semester's project outline, and groaned. "We are so not sleeping."

"Definitely not sleeping." Falcon slipped into the seat on my other side as the lecturer walked past and tapped our heads in a display that broke all campus rules, not that he cared in the least.

"And that's your three." He moved on to the next trio seated beside us, already scribbling our names down on his sheet. "And your three—"

"—Wait," I called, but he had already moved further along the row.

My protest was lost in the hubbub that arose from the plethora of chattering students suddenly keen on their project for one day before their collective interest waned.

Margot stopped before us, her mouth hanging open as she waved a finger in our direction, encircling all of us seated guiltily together. "What is happening here?"

I shrugged through my semi-discomfort at being encompassed by Dex's friends and sank deep in my seat, stuffed between the lordling and Mister Mafia. "Fucked if I know. They just turned up."

Margot huffed. "So much for dorm solidarity."

She turned on her heel and flounced off to the lower rows the lecturer hadn't made it to yet in search of group mates.

I spotted one of her prior one night stands that she linked her arms around and kissed on both cheeks. The poor dude threw his dreads over his shoulder in fright at the unexpected contact. I didn't blame him; she did kind of blindside the poor man. He seemed welcoming after his initial scare, and my guilt over not being able to work with her on this project eased a fraction.

I sighed, resolving myself to the conundrum of Dex's housemates apparently attaching themselves to my course and to me for the remainder of the semester. At least they seemed not to be too grumpy and were decent eye candy. And Dex would kick their respective asses if they got out of line. *Bonus.*

"Alright. I have ideas." I glanced at both of the boys, and bit my lip as my brain kicked into gear. "Do... either of you want to go first?"

Falcon watched me with his mouth shut tight. Nelson's eyes glittered.

This isn't freaking weird at all.

I let out a breath and went for it. "We rebrand the oldest fraternity on campus." I nibbled my lip, knowing Dex would hate my plan, mostly because I was about to do what I'd told him not to do when realistically I had no right to tell him not to do anything at all.

I was going to poke the bear.

"We're going to rebrand the Kingsman House."

And we were going to make it stick.

CHAPTER EIGHT

DEX

Zinzi worked at my cramped kitchen table with my roommates giving them utter hell for not keeping up with her brain. It was the sexiest thing I'd ever seen in my life. I'd never thought that seeing her take on two of the biggest bad asses—and Nelson definitely qualified after he barely flinched during the twins' torture, at least in my books—would do it for me, but there was no denying that seeing Zin sass out a foreign lord and a mafia heir boiled my blood.

Falcon pointed something out that stalled my girl for a moment. I pretended to work on my fake case as catch up work while I creeper-peeked at her over my laptop screen, waiting on her reaction. I wasn't the only one. Falcon had baited her, waited to see if she would arc up—still a fail in his eyes—or crumble under pressure. Nelson appeared poised to jump in and take the brunt of Falcon's pending outburst, whatever trap he thought he'd set for my girl.

Tension built in my spine, but I forced myself to relax. Zin could handle herself with these two. It was why I'd set her up with them int he first place—so that she had someone, or two someones—to watch her back while I was out of commission, thanks to Beau's fucked up version of fun.

And they'd done an admirable job, getting under her skin and weaseling their way into her classes so she never had to walk anywhere on her own, regardless of if the sun was up or not.

Zin didn't disappoint, either. She twirled her pencil in her hand, reaching out to flick Falcon's notes over and scribbled something on the back. He stared at whatever she had written for a second, then let out a bark of a laugh. She flipped him off.

He ruffled her hair.

I stared.

Nelson settled back in his seat with a smarmy grin on his face like all was motherfucking well with the world, and it was because of him when, as far as

I could tell, the bow tie twirling dick hadn't done a single damn thing.

I doubted Zinzi had any idea that simple, sassy motion would have earned anyone else a quick double tap and a pair of matching new breathing holes in their forehead from the handgun that lived in Falcon's silk wool blend suit jacket he'd hung carelessly over the back of his chair. Nor did I have any intention of telling her.

Still, I was proud of her for coming out of her shell and socializing in a situation that wasn't exactly her pick of friendship groups. From what Nelson told me they'd effectively butted her roomie out of her group project, and seconded Zin away. Not that she'd put up that much of a fight the way my boys told the tale.

My hand flexed inside the plasticky sheath that held my pinky in place. My ribs were declared successfully knitted together the week before, though fragile after a follow up x-ray, and my hand was close to coming out from its temporary cast. Everything still ached, but what hurt most was my heart. Call me lovelorn, depressed, what the fuck ever. I didn't care. What I wanted—or who—was the girl seated at our shitty little table that only just fit the three of us. Not the five we'd suddenly become.

I mulled on that, knowing the tiny dorm room Nelson and Falcon shared with me wasn't the right size any longer. Hell, we'd known that for a while. And we could have afforded better, every one of us, but we had chosen this existence because until recently, it kept us all off the radar.

At least, that had been the hope. Not hiding, exactly, just keeping a low profile.

Apparently, those days were over.

Well and truly over, as a faint knock that preceded Bella, Falcon's blonde, pretty girlfriend who he'd brought back with him from his beach town getaway, walked into our dorm room, towing a lithe young man behind her that seemed to be about Falcon's age.

"Rose, this is Zin, Nelson and D– Dex," she stuttered my name out, sliding her arms around Falcon's waist while still clinging to Rose's hand.

The heroin chic man with sallow skin and dark hair looked like he'd stepped straight out of a European fashion magazine, and seemed twice as uncomfortable as any of us in the cramped space.

I raised both eyebrows at his look and the way Bella clung to him and Falcon. Zin twisted in her seat to meet my eyes, a question of her own in her dipped brow. I shrugged, then nodded when Falcon kissed Bella first, then turned his head and found Rose's lips with his own. The lithe man melted at the mafia prince's attention, folding into his chest and making indecent sounds.

"Two guesses where this is headed." I shoved my laptop aside, holding out my hand.

Zin didn't ask questions as she gripped the edge of my cast gently, throwing a red-faced Nelson an apologetic look and followed me into my bedroom where I kicked the door shut behind her.

"That was...phew." Zin fanned her face, scanning my room.

She had flat out refused to enter my space since she'd started visiting me in my dorm under duress. I hadn't pushed the issue, but now that she was here....

"Zin," I murmured, leaning past her to flick the lock on my door, not wanting interruptions, but she wasn't watching me.

Her gaze soaked in my desk, the dark wood bed with its black cover, black pillows, black throw. Everything was cotton or wool because I fucking hated silky shit near my skin, unless it was attached to Zin's. The walls were painted black. I'd done that myself in my first year, shortly after I met her. The carpet was hidden beneath a plush black rug that ran the exact dimensions of the room, edge to edge. No other color entered the room, not through the thick, black drapes, apart from the thin sliver of light that slipped in because I hadn't sealed them in full.

Her sharp intake left me with one hand on her waist.

"Are you okay?"

"Funny time to discover I might be claustrophobic," she muttered.

"Need air?"

She nodded. I crossed the room and flung the window wide, but she put a hand on my arm when I went to throw the curtains open.

"Leave them," she whispered. "I don't want to destroy your space. That's why I didn't come in here in the first place."

I turned back to her and found her close. Really fucking close. Enough that my body brushed hers as I completed my revolution, standing chest to chest with her. One of the things I loved about Zin was that she was tall enough that I only had to dip my head to kiss her.

My hands landed on her waist, and I squeezed gently, cast and all. "I thought you didn't want to come in here because you thought we'd spend all our time fucking.," I growled, leaning in to reduce her air, stealing some of her sweet breath for myself.

Fuck, we hadn't been intimate for weeks, and having her this close was death.

Intoxicating.

"That, too," she acknowledged, swaying in my hold.

I swallowed hard. "You gonna let me kiss you?"

A slight huff escaped her lips. "At least you don't smell like blood and spew this time."

A grimace twisted my lips. "I'm sorry. I shouldn't have called you." *But I didn't want anyone else.*

Her hand came up and slapped my chest. My grimace became a wince. She shook her head.

"Don't you dare fake me, Dex Breaker. I was there when the doctor declared you fit. Not to fight but for...other things." She looked up at me through her lashes.

Thick lashes that curled at the ends. The last time she looked at me like that, it was with my cock stuffed down her throat.

Hell, if that wasn't an invitation, I didn't know what qualified.

"Zin?" I let her name hang between us for a full second before her eyes drifted shut and her head tipped back.

I squeezed her waist tight, ignored the ache that shot through my hand and pulled her flush into me, slamming my mouth over hers. The sound that ripped from her the moment our lips touched was hot and feral and everything I fucking needed. Jerking myself off each night with my left hand to the vision of her on her back beneath me was nowhere near close enough to the real thing.

Hell, I've missed you, sweetness.

I didn't know if those words came out of my mouth or simply echoed around my head, but they were loud and clear between my ears anyway. Having her in my arms as I plunged my tongue into her mouth like I was eating her pussy while she moaned worse than Falcon's extra little playmate?

That hit all the right notes.

I let out a groan of my own when I tried to lift her and couldn't because of the suffocating pressure that encased my lungs. Her hand slapping my chest added to the pain. I released her, swearing up a storm.

"I'm fucking useless."

"Yeah, because of some stupid bet or whatever that you made. Shut up, I don't want to hear it. Sit." She pointed to my bed, reaching for the hem of her top and pulled it over her head.

"No bra," I muttered when the expanse of her perfect, soft skin and dusky nipples filled my line of sight. "No panties, too?" I asked, hopefully.

She gave my chest another push. "Lie down, Dex."

I sat, more from her momentum than anything else, and kicked off my boots as she did the same and peeled her jeans from her body.

Nope, no panties.

My mouth dried. "How long have you not been wearing underwear to my place?"

She smirked. "Every single day, Dex. Does that visual do it for you?" She grabbed my jeans at the knees when I struggled and pulled them down, leaving me in my socks and jocks.

"Yeah. Everything about you does it for me. Fuck." I let my head fall back onto my pillow when her hand coasted over my dick. She rubbed me through the soft cotton and squeezed hard, then added her mouth to the combination, breathing hot air onto my balls. "Christ, girl. You're gonna kill me."

"Mmm. Maybe that's the goal."

My jocks disappeared. A naked Zin straddled me, rubbing her glorious bald pussy over my leaking dick. "Fuck, you're wet. Being in control is new for you, huh?"

I always led in our interactions. It never hit me that she might want to dominate, but today was the day I let that switch happen.

Zin's sexy as fuck smile left me groaning as she glided her soaked pussy lips over my dick and back again. Her fingers worked her clit in light circles. "I know you like to watch. So watch."

We'd made a game of masturbating in front of each other one night, both of us drunk as hell in our first year as fuck buddies. I learned that night she could come from nipple stimulation alone, and that four of her fingers could fit in her own pussy, but that without rubbing her clit she wouldn't get off from the penetration alone, at least, not if I wasn't buried deep inside her.

And she learned that she loved me coming on her. The taint made us both feel dirty as hell. We fucked for hours afterward, both of us smeared in my cum and insane with lust for each other.

That last factor never really abated. Just like now.

I held myself still—in part to reduce the pain when I breathed, laid out on my back, an action that still ached in the wrong position, and partly because I knew that was what she needed today. To be in control and for me to keep my hands off her, at least for now.

Let her play.

Her fingers dipped, alternating between rubbing her clit and seeking out the beads of precum that leaked from the tip of my dick. I released a repressed groan as she teased me.

"How long do you expect me to hold out?" I asked quietly. "Because watching you touch yourself and me while you're riding me…"

I wanted to close my eyes and just feel her, but I couldn't take my eyes off the pleasure written across her face, the way her pert breasts, not too big, sat high. I risked trailing my hands along her thighs, keeping away from her pussy. She let me, watching with hooded eyes as her breath came faster. I reached for her breasts, tracing circles around her darkened areolas, until her breasts grew heavier in my hands. Her pants came faster and she rocked her hips in time with my touch.

"That's it," I whispered. "Come for me, sweetness. Flood me with your cream. You gonna lap it up for me later, or leave me sticky with your mess?" I liked both options, but I knew talking dirty would get her there faster.

Her breath hitched and I drew my fingers across her nipples lightly, not offering any pinches or pain, just stroked down her engorged, over sensitized flesh.

Zin came, shuddering and gushing and messy as fuck all over my cock, and I wasn't even inside her yet. Her thighs trembled and her pretty mouth opened just wide enough that I knew if I flipped her, my dick would sink right to the back of my throat.

I knew this girl, exactly how her body worked, and I loved every inch of her.

Not letting my needs take over I kept circling my fingertips lightly around her nipples, knowing she'd come again fast from here. It only took one orgasm and she was ready to go again and again. With Zin, the key was to not stop. Her hips knew the program, still rocking on my length. I nudged my knees up, and it was an easy slide inside her tight, but swollen, drenched hole.

Her moan reverberated off my black room walls. I prayed her voice soaked into my dorm room for good, willing the echoes of her orgasm to imprint on my brain so I could hear her over again later. Her pussy walls clenched down on my again and again as I teased her nipples while her body did the rest, sliding all the way down on my thick length until her bare pussy lips rested against my waxed balls.

"Look how well you take me," I whispered,

gently pinching her nipples. "Split open and stretched so well, like you'll let me ruin you forever. Ride me Zin," I begged, my ego not inflated enough to prevent my asking her to take us home.

Dozy, lust-fucked eyes framed with thick, curly lashes met mine as she nodded.

Zin followed the command I knew she wanted anyway as I held onto her nipples, milking her as she started to climax again, using my pincer grip to bring her slamming back down onto my dick. Her shattered scream choked in her throat. My balls drew up but I willed the orgasm back, and by some miracle, it worked.

"Once more," I murmured, though I wasn't sure she heard me.

Her thighs trembled beautifully as she rode me, her body shaking with the force of each thrust I met her with, each tremor a mini orgasm of its own. She milked my dick with her perfect hot, soaked pussy the way I milked her nipples.

When her pink tongue slipped out of her mouth, the thinnest bead of saliva dripped from the tip to land on the place where my dick met her pussy. My next thrust pushed the glossy bead inside her, and I came with a shout. Pain and pleasure mingled with the force of my climax as I filled her, pumping her with enough cum that I coated her pussy lips with a few extra thrusts.

My hands slapped down onto her hips, needing her not to clean up and keep her marked with my fluids for a while longer.

"Don't move, sweetness," I muttered. "Stay here with me."

She let me wrap my arms around her, nestling into the crook of my neck like that was exactly where she was meant to be.

And for a short period, until she slithered off my body and left me aching for her again, we both knew it.

CHAPTER NINE

ZINZI

"It can come off." The doctor freed Dex's hand from the blue cast with a flourish. "You're cleared. But if I see you again, I'll inject something illegal into you." The joking look in the medical practitioner's eyes was only slightly humorous.

Somehow, I felt like he knew more about this situation than I did.

Dex flexed his hand and shook it out. Fresh new dark lines of ink I didn't remember being on that hand decorated his wrist. Not that fresh, because his flesh didn't bear the telltale tinge of red that his other tattoos had when he got those fresh or kept them under plastic wrap. I frowned, but he shifted before I could make out the image on his skin.

"Thanks, Doc. Appreciate your work."

"Hmm." The doctor grunted and cleared him with a slip for college. "That should cover you for any assignments for another two weeks. Not that you'll need it with that brain of yours. But just in case."

"Extra appreciation." Dex winked, grabbed my hand with his now good one, and squeezed. "Ready to go home?"

My stomach tumble turned. "Uh—"

He grinned and leaned in. "This is the part where you say *yes*."

But *yes* had never been a big part of my repertoire. Ask his roommates who were currently butting heads with me over the branding group project. Mind, they had Shanghaied me into their little soiree trio, so they also got to wear the consequences.

"Alright?" I smiled weakly and waved to the doctor who watched us leave with no small amount of concern on his lined face.

I was certain Dex had added several of those lines himself. I knew I had an extra *something* from him. Stress. Panic. Fear.

Orgasms.

I was still in recovery mode from our last session

in his bedroom where I had actually fallen asleep on his chest, even if *asleep* counted as a doze of about ten minutes. When I crept out and Dex still snored on, Falcon and his entourage were still hard at it in his room while a sweaty and disheveled looking Nelson stared fixedly at his phone in the living room.

I didn't see his hands, and I didn't dare ask where they were as I slipped out of their door and shut it quietly behind me, though I doubted my exit went entirely unnoticed.

Certainly not by Dex, who messaged me less than an hour later, begging me to come back.

And I nearly—so freaking close—had.

But I didn't. I held to my resolve and stayed clear of his toxic little household and my toxic more-than-a-fuck-buddy who was becoming way too close for comfort.

Or maybe just too close all over, because those orgasms felt so damn fine. My legs trembled all the way back across campus.

And now I knew what it was like to be the one doing the walk of shame. Not that it was the walk that bothered me so much, but who was watching. And during daylight hours, that seemed to be... everyone.

Now, taking Dex back to his dorm in my tiny car

that seemed even smaller with him inside it, I had no idea what to say. Six weeks into our new found friendship and I was still at a loss for words beside him unless we were in the bedroom or the sun had set.

Because preferences.

"You know you don't have to run off on me. We could have lunch," Dex suggested, sliding his good arm across my shoulders as I drove.

I twitched. "Uh, distraction, much. You." I shot him a glance and looked back at the road. "And I have a ton of work to catch up on because I've been playing nurses and doctors with someone."

"Now there's a fantasy I could get into. We could buy outfits."

I groaned. "Of course that's where you go with it. I don't do skirts, Dex."

He snorted. "Always with the assumptions. What if *I* wanted to wear the nurse's outfit, huh? I've got a good chest, pecs and all." He emphasized his barrel chest, pushing it out and wiggling suggestively in my passenger seat.

I burst into giggles. "You're madness."

He put on a puppy face, fluttering his lashes for me. "You know it."

"And we're here." Thankfully, because I couldn't

do any more of this easy chat stuff. My heart was pounding in my chest and I needed a breather. Which couldn't happen with Dex in the car, him being the sole reason for my inability to gain a lung full of fresh air. "Is this how you felt when you had cracked ribs?" I pressed a hand to my side and squeezed.

Rather than evict him from my undersized car, the motion only brought him closer. "Zin? What happened?" His arms folded around me in an unbreakable circle.

I shook my head, but he refused to back off, insisting on turning my face toward him. "Stop, please," I whispered, but he was right there, and too close.

Way too close.

"Talk to me," he insisted. "Are you having a panic attack? What do you need?"

"Air. I need air—"

"Sweetness," he murmured, releasing my seatbelt and yanking up my parking brake in one go—the pros of two working hands, look he could use them both at once to my supposed benefit again for me—and cupped my face, stealing more of my air. *Again.*" Talk to me?"

I shoved at his chest with both hands, and some

of the breath burst out of him. "It's you," I yelled, needing the space. "Just back *off*, Dex!" I ran my hands through my hair, pushing loose strands off my face, the ends intent on itching everything, *everywhere*.

Hurt rippled over his face. "Okay," he said slowly, leaning back in the passenger seat, his hands raised. "I'm back here. Wanna tell me what that was?" He spoke low and slow, like I was some dangerous animal he wasn't sure he should be worried about or not.

Maybe he should avoid me. Maybe that had been the problem all along.

"I can't do this," I whispered. "All the, the domestication. Sitting with your friends. Playing happy families. It's not like I have one."

"I know," Zin," he said quietly.

The single topic we both shied away from, because we matched in that respect. I didn't have a family to claim me, period, hence the poor girl in a rich boy world problem. His remaining family passed away in his first year before we bonded enough that he could share his grief with me. My throat still closed on the thought of him going through that without anyone at all. Because I didn't know how to deal with it, never having anyone.

So I guessed that was a good reason that I found out months later, through a rumor on campus. And then...I still didn't talk to him about it, because back then that's not who we were. And my rules kept that relationship in place.

I shook my head, throwing off the broken memory. "It's too much, Dex. This...Us. It's killing me. Please." One hot tear dropped onto my cheek but I was too lost in my head to care that he watched me cry.

Not a damn thing changed on his face as one tear fell after another. Not a single thing. It was like he was made of concrete. A brick wall.

"Okay." He rolled his lips inward and nodded. "Why don't you stop the car, and come in? We can have something to eat."

"I'm not eating with you, Dex, and I'm not coming inside," I forced the words out through clenched teeth.

"Alright. A walk?" His eyes hooded, his whole body stilled.

I wondered if this was what he was like right before a fight when he shut down everything that mattered and only left the necessary bits running.

"Please get out." I kept my tone polite by some miracle. "I need to go home and just be—"

"Be what?" His voice came out harsh, showing emotion for the first time.

"Just *be*, Dex. Me. You're suffocating me."

If the hurt that rippled over his face before sank my stomach, it was nothing to what I saw on his face now. The man who moved before me might as well never have had cracked ribs, and if the ones in his body offered any residual pain at all he ignored it right now, sliding out of my car and slamming the door.

Before I exhaled my next breath he was gone, striding into his dorm building. That door slammed behind him, too. I fumbled my phone, my fingers dancing over the keys on a single sentence that I deleted six times before I finally sent anything at all.

ZINZI: See you next Friday.

I waited for a long moment, too long a moment before the three dots appeared as he read the words that hadn't been my first choice but turned out to be the only choice I could send to him.

Then the dots disappeared and were replaced by his message that I didn't want to read at all.

DEX: *Don't worry about it.*

I fumbled to open my calendar, but by the time I found the app, every Friday night block that had

Dex's name on it right through to graduation and beyond was cleared.

Damnit, I should have just gone with I'm sorry.

But I hadn't, and so I drove home with eyes full of tears, realizing that I hadn't asked about the new ink etched along his arm beneath the cast I'd spotted when the doctor took it off that shouldn't have been able to be there at all.

CHAPTER TEN

ZINZI

Dex wasn't coming, just like he promised.

At least, not with me.

I waited at home on my Friday night for over two hours, pining until Margot called in what should have been the middle of my fuck fest, her usual self completely okay with being ignored while I got Dex out of my system right up until I bawled all over her through the phone instead.

Less than an hour later she had me topped up with tequila, primped and primed with an amount of makeup I'd have to chisel from my face come tomorrow morning, and dressed in a little red beaded number that barely covered my butt cheeks and shimmered to purple whenever I moved.

"I never even got to wear it," Margot mourned, sipping her oversized espresso vodka from a Rippton U branded tumbler. Then her expression brightened. "But fuck him. Let's make you the wet dream of every student on campus."

With that goal in mind, I let her drag me from each sorority party to the next dorm, and finally to the Kingsman's house. Their current branding still stood proud against the architraves. I swore, in my tipsy state, that I would fix that listing lion with its frazzled mane before the end of semester, or bust.

The night passed me in a blur for a period until I found myself leaning against one wall of the house, inside the frat party trying not to think of what might have been done against said wall in the past and attempted to blend in.

Spoilers: I failed.

Horrifyingly.

Not only did I *not* manage to blend in, but I blended so poorly that after my roomie tried to drag me out onto the impromptu and alcohol fueled dance floor, knocking back three approaches from frat boys and one girl who wandered up to us both with a kissy face—kudos to Margot; the dress *worked* —I found myself nose-to-nose with the Lord of the All.

AKA Nelson Milton, complete with a private boy's school blazer that he didn't attend and a sporting powder blue bowtie. Combined with shiny black patent shoes, tan slacks ironed within an inch of their lives and a pompadour hairstyle that might have gone out of style sometime in the last century —not the nineteen hundreds—he managed to pull it all off in a sexy, *I'll never hurt you, Lass,* type of way.

The Earl of Nothingness—self-proclaimed, not my words—watched me sway on my chosen patch of soggy carpet in my borrowed heels with a careful eye.

"Are you going to stand there all night, you Brit perv?" I nudged his thigh with my knee playfully to take the edge off my words, forgetting I wore a skirt for the first time in God only knew how long.

Highschool, probably. I blamed the tequila and my roommate as I smoothed the beaded material nervously, ducking to hide behind my hair curtain as he returned my scrutiny.

Not that I was uncomfortable with Nelson. I'd become more than familiar with both him and Falcon in the last months, working with them side by side. Thankfully, neither of them slacked off, though I suspected that last was because of some unspoken threat that came direct from Dex. Even if we weren't speaking, he still made an effort to protect me.

The suffocation factor doubled.

"He thought I might find you here." Nelson brought up the beast not in the room and bestowed me with his sweetest smile all at once, throwing a pair of the cutest dimples my way.

He was seriously gorgeous, if you were into that sort of thing.

I needed far more grit, and maybe a few bruises to make it all work for me, but hey, I got it. Nelson looked like he hadn't taken a single punch in his life. Or done anything with his hands. There were girls who liked that kind of thing, I guessed.

I kinda liked rough fingers. And grit. And ink. And broken things.

Which brought me back to Dex.

The very missing Dex from my bed who broke our agreement and my rules, which made me super snappy, especially when my shitty mood was paired with tequila.

"He who?" I shot back at Nelson, but with no heat.

We both knew who he meant.

"Pet." Nelson looked at me sorrowfully. He trailed a hand down my face and leaned forward.

"He's loitering behind the pillar, lamenting the fact he brushed you off today like the natural asshole he is. Wanna bring out the beast?" His gray eyes sparkled with undiluted mischief.

Perhaps the Lord of Nothing at All is more interesting than I gave him credit for.

I grinned at his sassy, toyboy smile. "You're on."

"You're not going to ask what I had in mind?" He pressed a hand over his heart and stumbled. "I'm mortally wounded, milady."

"You're a giant flirt is what you are, Lord Nelson." I flipped my hair and laughed at his theatrics, my chest loosening enough that I managed to breathe for the first time in hours.

Since I realized Dex had blown me off.

I'll blow something, but it won't be you, baby.

The concept of revenge, no matter how petty, spurred me on.

"Call me that between the sheets and I'll rise to full mast for you." Nelson wiggled his eyebrows until his pompous hair flopped boyishly over his eyes.

I burst out laughing as he leaned both arms above me, resting his forearms either side of my head to cage me in against my chosen section of wall. *Maybe the Lord of Nothingness has more muscle than I expected.* Who knew what a knit vest, a good bow tie, and a blazer could hide?

The mood between us sobered in an instant. I crooked one leg against the wall, tilting my head back. *Who's the fucking flirt here?*

But teasing Dex—when he either walked away still wanting me or didn't want me at all—with a man he knew was all too tempting.

I trailed my tongue across my bottom lip, watching Nelson's pupils dilate as his gaze followed the motion.

"Pity this is only a one-time thing," he murmured. "Mourn my loss, Zinzi. He'll tan my hide for touching you."

Dex.

Guilt slapped me face first as my tequila-addled brain realized what we were about to do and what a really bad idea this was for both of us.

He cancelled everything. He didn't turn up.

Did that mean we had broken up? Were we ever together? I didn't remember making that agreement with him. We were fuck buddies, then I was nursing him—under duress, and he hosted a group project at a place not of my choosing—also under duress, because his housemates seemed to coerce me into working with them.

So, we were never really together. Had we ever broken up?

Does it matter?

My head argued it didn't. My heart hurt like hell. And then Nelson's mouth was on mine, and all choice was removed from the equation. I didn't have a chance to push him for more.

The Lord of the Moment dove in like he planned on devouring me, but in reality he kept his kiss light, a gentle pressure of lips on lips, grazing over each other in an undeniably intimate touch. He tasted like hops and lime, whatever fruity craft beer he'd been drinking. When his tongue lightly probed the seam of my lips, I parted them, giving him permission.

Then I found out what kissing a Lord was really like.

One hand cupped the back of my head, his other firm on my jaw, angling me the way he wanted as his tongue danced along mine. I shivered, remembering this was all to tease Dex, to show him what he didn't have right now. But I couldn't help thinking how lucky the girl would be who Nelson kissed like he truly loved her.

The man must be a mini-God on the sorority girl

campus circuit. I promised myself I'd find out if his bed game was as good as his tongue game.

After that I never found out more as cold air met my lips because when I reached for him, my hands came up empty.

Well, empty at first.

Then my palms hit a hard chest, tangling in a shirt that elicited a scent of sin and sweat that I knew better than anything else.

"Dex," I whispered, my voice too soft to be heard over the thumping house music.

My eyes cracked open, lazy like I'd been kissing him instead of his friend, to find the man I loved to hate not to date most staring back at me with unyielding eyes.

Why Nelson or I thought teasing this deadly, obsessive man would be fun, I had no idea.

We made a really big mistake.

"Dex, mate. We were about to come looking for you." Nelson narrowed his eyes at me over Dex's shoulder before the man in question turned on his friend and Nelson's smile widened, his expression guileless in the face of impending doom. "She tastes good. Want to share?"

I shook my head frantically as Nelson touched his lips that were stained red with the remnants of my lip gloss. When he held that finger out to Dex I groaned, closing my eyes. I didn't need to watch what happened next to know the first thump heralded Dex's fist connecting with Nelson's aristocratic nose, and the second was his roommate hitting the Kingsman's floor.

Then I was yanked away from the door and dragged through the crowd that parted before us without question. His face must have been terrible, because not a single soul questioned Dex, or offered to halt his path. I sent up a singular prayer for Nelson's continued existence as I plucked at the steel-like fingers wrapped around my wrist.

"Dex—" I gasped, stumbling a little as the copious amount of tequila Margot poured into me before we hit the Friday night frat parties left me dizzier with every stride that exceeded the natural length of my own.

"Not a fucking word," Dex snapped at me over his shoulder.

If his words didn't shut me up, the abject betrayal and hurt laced in his tone did.

The last time I spoke to him, I hurt him, too.

I hung my head and let him tow me out of the party after that without a word. Fresh, chill air brushed my cheeks as he drew me out through the front door, but we didn't stop there. Dex's rough grip slipped from my arm. His thumb massaged the spot where he had gripped me firm but not too tight a moment before and trailed to my hand, closing his fingers around my fingers.

A question was in that touch that I wasn't sure either of knew the answer to right then. A question he'd been seeking an answer for over the last weeks.

I wasn't any more ready to provide him with what he sought tonight than I had been earlier in the week or any of the weeks I came to his house to care for him. My heart beat a faint staccato in my chest, like it, too, held out hope that I'd find something I knew I couldn't give. His thumb brushed over my wrist in gentle caress so different to his dominating nature that his touch drew my heart into my throat.

"I'm sorry," I whispered again, choking on the apology for wanting to hurt him.

For wanting revenge at being lonely and missing him when I was the one who pushed him away in the first place.

Seeing the pain in his eyes put everything into perspective. He walked away from me because I couldn't give him what he wanted, and in revenge I gave away what he claimed. We might pretend to hate each other, but somewhere along the line the H-word turned into the unspoken L-word...and I missed that.

Or maybe I just couldn't accept that he loved me and what that might mean that I would have to commit to. What scared me so much when he was right in front of me the entire time.

But the way he touched me now, the tightness in his features as he stared at my just-kissed lips, only not by him...that hurt more than anything else.

I betrayed him, and now he might never want to come back.

Dex drew me into a shadowy area away from the house and paused next to an ancient oak. Its trunk was wider than his oversized shoulders. A flick of his wrist, and I found my back pressed against its thick girth. The rough bark caught on the beaded dress, sending red glitter pinging in all directions as my skirt rode up.

His hand clamped down on my hip in a possessive move that left me panting. A breath later, he crowded my space. His hands released me to cup my face as his thighs pressed to mine, his fathomless, tortured gaze seeking answers in my own.

"Why did you do it? Because it hurt when I wasn't there? Or did you just have a tantrum and decide I wasn't worth your time anymore? That *we* aren't worth it?" He shot question after question at me, not waiting for answers we both knew I wouldn't give him anyway. "You asked about sharing one time. Is that what you want? What do I need to do to keep you, Zin? Offer you what Falcon has?"

It was on the tip of my tongue to throw his words back at him, to say that there was no *we* and never had been. But that wasn't the truth, and if this was the last time he touched me, then he deserved my shredded version of honesty, and everything that I'd been hiding from myself behind a veil of lust while I fell in love by accident.

"I made a mistake," I whispered, staring up at his hard face, the way his gaze searched mine until I trembled in his hands under his intensity, knowing he could be so much worse, but wasn't. What did that mean? "I hurt when you didn't come back. I mean, I know it's my fault—" My apology fractured when he made a feral, violent sound through his teeth. I closed my eyes and pushed on, regardless. "You're right. I wanted you to hurt too. But I wanted to get a reaction, anything out of you for leav—" I choked on a sob, my cheeks cold and coated in salt and regret. "For abandoning me. Because this is what I *didn't want*, Dex. I didn't *want* to care." I shoved at his chest as his face blurred. "I didn't want to fall for– for–"

Dex watched me flounder on in silence, and this unspeaking version of him was worse than if he'd yelled curses at me.

"You," I finished in a whisper.

No amount of tequila could numb the pain that sliced through me at that last admission. I'd tried to hide my truth from him and myself when I'd lied to both of us in saying I hated him. I didn't get attached because it hurt, but here we were, not attached by omission, and it hurt all the same. Far too much.

Dex, the Heart Breaker. Just like I expected when I made the rules so he wouldn't stay, and I wouldn't end up like this.

Again.

I leaned my head back against the tree, my eyes closed to avoid dealing with the raw turmoil roiling behind his eyes.

"Nu-uh, Zin. You look at me when you apologize. I need to know that you hurt as bad as I do right now," he grated the words out through white lips. "I need to know if your games are finished."

If we are finished.

He didn't say it, and neither did I. There was a finality to those words. Forming them felt too real, like maybe we couldn't take them back if either one of us said them. I shook my head, opening my eyes like he demanded, but instead of looking at him, I stared up into the underside of the oak's broad canopy.

Because I couldn't bear to look at him only to see my own fears reflected back at me. Right now that brought reality too close.

I wanted to go back to kissing the Lord of Nothingness in the party and pretending we could do what we wanted. I wanted to be a drunk wallflower who nobody saw. I wanted to be the girl with the broken heart, hiding from the man she thought wasn't looking for her, because anything was better than this.

No you don't.

Or I could keep lying to myself like I had for the last two and a half years since I first met Dex and fell head over heels for him when I pretended I didn't.

"Seeing someone else kiss you fucking ripped my soul apart. No one else should taste you like I do. But if you want to hurt, baby, then I can provide that." Dex's thumbs brushed away my tears, his warm breath so close it dried the tracks on my cheeks. "Close your eyes, Zin, and *feel*." His mouth slanted over mine, he kissed me, hard and deep and all the things that Dex was.

But this was...different. Not rough, not playful. His touch was possessive, knowing me. But also asking a question.

I knew the answer, but I couldn't bring myself to say it.

Even if it meant this was our last kiss.

His tongue tasted every part of my mouth, denying the touch of another man, erasing Nelson's fake kiss as he replaced it with one of his own, though nothing about Dex was fake. It never had been. He was the real thing, no matter how many times I denied that to myself and to him. He saw it. He knew, and he tried so hard to tell me.

But I kept running. Because I'd been hurt, and I never wanted to be owned. Having someone consider me their possession terrified me, right up until the moment when I thought I lost Dex, and he showed me exactly what I was missing in denying him those sleepovers, breakfasts, morning cuddles meant. The dates he begged me to share.

The lunches. Walks.

My knees buckled as Dex drew away, my back sliding down the length of the ancient trunk until my butt hit the cold, unforgiving ground with no knowing hands to hold me up.

Because when I opened my eyes, Dex was gone and the only familiar figure I recognized was Nelson loping across the frat house yard. His pale gray eyes were tired, and an icepack was pressed to his jaw. He slid down the trunk next to me, offering a comfort I couldn't take because he wasn't the man I wanted.

I turned my head to the side, curled my knees to my chest, and let my heart break beneath the shadow of a tree who stood firm at my back.

I just wished it was Dex instead.

CHAPTER ELEVEN

DEX

I canceled the following Friday night fuck session with Zinzi the moment she threw me out of her car and went straight to knocking out my testosterone in the cage the next day, doctor's orders be damned. At least, that was the original plan. The plan before Nelson and my girl decided it would be fun to fuck with me.

Look how well that worked out.

Not once in my two and a half years at Rippton U had I not spent my Friday night worshiping her body until I let Beau Bennett break me with his goddam fight rules, and when he did, Zin was there for me. We met on our first day of college—thank you orientation week for setting me up with the most gorgeous hottie on campus—at the union bar. She took one look, propositioned me and, well. Why give up on a good thing?

The problem was that now I wanted *more*. I always had with her, but I'd bided my time, earned her trust—or so I thought—and worked my way into her heart. Right up until she threw me out. Again and again, pushing me away. Anyone else might have taken that as a sign she didn't want me but I knew this girl, and I knew why.

She was scared.

We never talked about her ex. The man who hurt her so bad she couldn't trust anyone else. I never asked, and she never volunteered information. But I didn't get the grades I did for no reason, and I didn't live with a billionaire and a mafia heir for shits and giggles.

One night's virtual stalking brought up everything I needed to know about Zinzi Jones in our first month together. I got curious about the girl I was shagging, and despite the rocking body she let me play with on a weekly basis, I knew those rules of hers had to come from somewhere.

And hell, did she have a reason to be scared.

One Ledger Raymond, currently serving a five-year sentence for essentially beating the shit out his girlfriend. He was also a fan of not so blunt trauma. It didn't take me long while I was providing Zin with an overdose of orgasms the next week—insisting on one small lamp on for 'ambience'—to find the faint lines where she'd been stitched back together.

He'd lost a good part of his inheritance thanks to her court case, and the plastic surgeon had done a great job, but he hadn't been able to remove all the evidence on her body for the damage that she had suffered at the asshole's hands.

I knew, and so I never pushed.

But I also refused to let her run from me just because I knew why she couldn't commit. I played by her rules every damn week, breaking a little more inside every time I left, unable to sleep beside her because every time she threw me out, I wanted to stay and hold her. I hurt for her, loved her a little more for what she couldn't face.

Until we hit here. Wherever the fuck *here* was.

And kissing her like I did that last night at the frat party, letting her know I really wanted her...that hurt as much as seeing another man's hands on her skin. A man I fucking knew.

Lord Nelson Milton was lucky he still has his entrails as in innards and not his outards. And he was lucky I liked him as a roommate. Hell, I even understood why he did what he did with her. I just enjoyed busting his nose up more.

But that didn't distract me from the girl who became the center of my growing obsession. I'd be lying if I said I hadn't craved more of Zin for a long damn time. More of what we had, more of her time. And it looked like we finally reached an impasse neither of us could compromise on in either direction.

I couldn't keep going with the meager time I stole from her while for the rest of the week my heart beat outside my chest, raw and breaking. She wasn't prepared to give us any more than a few hours before midnight once classes finished up for the week.

That still drove me insane on several levels even if I understood her *why*. Instead of pounding my need out into her body, taking her home and reminding her why we were perfect together, I slammed my fist over and over and over into the unknown man's face until he was slightly less than recognizable, Beau Bennett's fucking fight rules be damned.

Fuck it, I'd get him a bumper sticker and we could call it a day. I was done.

The ref, always good for a bloodbath as long as

he didn't have to get his pretty, unmarked hands dirty, called time but I couldn't stop. We didn't have a standing eight count; when a man couldn't get up, the fight was done. But my mind didn't want to play by those rules tonight.

Too many fucking rules and I'm done with them all.

Somewhere in my periphery, I noticed the twins' blond heads leave the arena. My brain may have switched off after that. Once the threat was gone I had no reason to do anything but what Jericho wanted: play up to the crowd and earn him money as recompense for the weeks I was off. I never did get to emcee, distracted by Zinzi.

And so the beatings continue.

Week after week. Saturday nights became Wednesday nights. Monday nights. What the hell was the point of anything if I worked around classes, without seeing Zin? Her soft and sassy touch seemed to have eased something in me that raged to the surface now, unchecked. My nails grew caked with blood and when the post ran out of room for extra marks, I let the ringside tattooist ink my skin instead.

I never chased Zin, and she never came to see me. The boys continued working with her, but they didn't meet up at ours. Even Falcon watched me with different eyes, but I didn't have time for him, either.

All I wanted was to work, study, and fight. Maybe Beau left a different door open the night he came into my home and started cutting up my friends and threatening the girl I loved.

Maybe he could be the next one in the cage with me.

Afterall, a count was a count.

Tonight was like any other night. The face before me splattered with blood that wasn't mine. Before the fight was over I could already feel the extra mark burn into my flesh. It had become such a ritual, almost daily at this point. Jericho yellowed something from the other side of the wire. I bared my teeth at him, spittle flying from my lips as I threw my boot into the man's ribs.

Something cracked, and the man groaned.

I sent him a smile that never reached my eyes. "Enjoy the healing process, my friend." I leaned down and punched him in the face.

Finally, the chicken-shit ref and his whistle got into the cage and yanked me off the man who blew bubbles in the blood pouring around his mouth. I barely managed to stop myself from nailing the ref as well, and I wasn't done yet. One of the busty bunnies who loitered at the cage door in hope of a sweaty lay with the victor handed me a towel.

I swiped the rag across my face and threw it back at her without a second glance, unwilling to see her plastic pout and thrust barely-concealed fake tits I didn't want into my face.

"Next."

And the next, and the next.

By the time I was done the cage had made more money than was reasonable for any regular Saturday night, even for an illegal cage fight, while I earned a few extra stripes etched into my arm. There were more scars under my name now than anyone else's, including the guys who'd been fighting on the regular for years. Dudes with more numbers in their age than I had seen summers, but I didn't give a shit.

"Next."

"You're done for the night." Jericho gave me a hard look and shoved an obscenely heavy wad of bills that I didn't need into my hands. He nodded toward the back area where I left my kit before we started hours ago. My limbs started to grow heavy without the constant deluge of chemicals from the ring that I'd programmed into myself day after day. "Clean up and get out. See you next week."

"Next week." Blood ran into the corner of my mouth from a cut I hadn't felt open.

Adrenaline still pulsed faintly through me,

raging in my blood. The shakes would set in soon, then the exhaustion. They might be done for the night, but I wasn't. I changed out of my running shorts and into my jeans, wiping my face with the towel.

I couldn't explain why the fuck I looked so beat up to any cop who might see me, so I popped my tee over my head to cover the bruises and bashing I'd taken in my pursuit of conquering fear and out distancing heartbreak.

Not that any of it worked. I still ached for Zin, craving her in dark and desperate ways. She used to pretend to hate me while I fucked her senseless once a week, pushing me away when I found her after class or in the library, and kissed her.

It still wasn't enough. Nowhere near fucking enough.

What had been enough was the knowledge that when I begged her for a date those cold eyes that only lit once a week when I was in her bed flamed for me right then. When I promised her I'd treat her right, that I wanted to screw her rules—and her—to the wall and wake with her in my arms every fucking morning, that pledge turned something on inside her. Something that she hid from herself.

When I found her again and kissed her under

the oak tree at the Kingsman House, erasing another man's taste from her lips, she kissed me back like she yearned for more. And then she cried, because though she thought I walked away, I stayed. I made sure as fuck Nelson got her home safe.

If he hadn't, he wouldn't be breathing right now. Not after what he started.

That night—it didn't start as a test, but it felt like one for both of us. That kiss wasn't real. We all knew that. But seeing her break for me when I faced off against her...I never wanted to see her hurt like that ever again.

When we talked about love and commitment, back when I kissed her in front of the campus knowing she'd hate the publicity stunt, I saw her eyes light. Then I saw the fear that shadowed the burn we had for each other. The man who hurt her before...I'd rip him limb from fucking limb and shove every one of his digits into a fresh orifice I tore apart with my own hands the moment he emerged from his cell. His punishment was far from done.

My feet walked the walk toward the exit on my behalf, heading around the ring like Jericho directed me. I'd feel every hit come at sunrise, but for now my system pumped with a numbing high that left me chasing inevitability. My shirt smelled like Zin the moment I put it on from the last time I'd been in her room, or maybe when she'd stayed with me for a brief time, sharing my space. When I'd last been inside *her*.

No matter what I did, no matter how many miles I ran or how many hard punches I threw, I couldn't be free of her.

Did I want to be free of Zinzi? No. I wanted to fuck her in her shower and crawl into her bed. I wanted to wrap my arms around her, worship her curves soft and breathe in her fucking delicious scent when she moaned beneath my battered body. I wanted to feel her mouth on mine and her dripping cunt wrapped around my cock while I made her scream for me in an admission that this—us—was so much more than just lust.

And I was hard again.

Painfully so. Some screwed up kink in me liked that I ached for her, that she denied me. My jeans strangled my cock, the denim already too tight with tonight's accumulated sweat and grit that shrank my pants a size too small. Night air assailed my swelling face as I pushed open the back door to the ramshackle building.

I spat a glob of saliva mixed with blood into the gutter outside the nondescript structure situated in a block of similar dingy warehouses and filthy, unlit alleys. After years of fighting here first weekly and now almost every night, the cage had started to feel like a second home.

Rather than catch the train back to campus, I decided to run my excess rage out into the pavement, but a vision of glossy black locks and painted red lips slammed into me like a derailed freight train.

Zinzi leaned against the back of the building like she'd known exactly where I'd exit the place after my fights.

Fuck me. I knew I saw her here.

That was months ago. Motherfucking *months*.

She'd known I was fighting all this time. That she'd known and lied to me didn't bother me because only one thought lingered at the front of my mind, freezing me in place.

This is the least safe place for her.

The twins might have left, my deal with Beau expired, or so it seemed, but that didn't mean she wasn't still on their crazy as fuck radar. My blood, still simmering, boiled afresh.

"You looked pretty impressive in there."

The girl who never wore skirts except when she was out to make a statement tugged a candy red lollipop out of her mouth to top off the delectable fucking image she made, her eyes focused only on me as her lips made a perfect 'o' the shape to match my cock.

No sign of the trembling girl whispering her apologies like the last time I saw her at the Kingsman frat party was in sight. I hadn't been able to see her since then in case I did something really stupid, like bend a knee and beg a lifetime of love and forgiveness from every inch of her bones.

Hell, I'd come close a dozen times or more in the last two weeks after she blocked me on her phone. Part of me thought I'd never talk to her again, never be able to drink in her stunning form again. She pushed me away plenty of times. After the frat party I finally got the message, loud and motherfucking clear.

And part of me thought I'd broken her. That I'd cowed her into who she was scared to be. Not who we were together. The ballsy, bratty girl who could take on the world when we were together.

Who took me on, at my worst. Who flipped off Falcon Gianio and lived. Who kissed a billionaire lord and walked away from him. The poor girl on campus who didn't give a shit about what brand of credit cards lay in a man's wallet. Hell, she was one of a kind, and I thought I'd ruined her.

I thought maybe I lost her forever, and I was all too ready to grovel so damn hard for the girl I hurt.

But now Zin was here, and she wasn't cowed at all. I liked that, because now she stood before me, unbroken, or at least, as unbroken as me, and I could play out every dark fantasy I wanted in this filthy alley with the girl I wanted so bad I ached.

When she was like this, I wasn't afraid to hurt her.

Her stretchy, black lace top had scalloped edges that caressed the gentle curve of her stomach and accentuated her cleavage, leaving a slim line of toned skin on display. Below the strip of bared flesh sat a tiny, sparkly skirt that brushed the top of her thighs and barely concealed her round ass. On her feet were her customary biker boots leaving her legs bare.

I raked my gaze over her, the fresh rush of adrenaline switching undiluted rage to instant desire. "What the fuck are you doing here?"

"Watching you." She sent me a sassy as fuck little smile and sucked the lollipop back into her mouth. Her lips wrapped around the cherry candy colored treat in a popping sound that left me hard and groaning. "Isn't that what you wanted? To spend more time together?"

I looked away from her. "You're pissed about that night." She didn't have to tell me, and I didn't have to look at her to see her eyes flash in defiance, or resentment maybe.

All the hurt in the last two weeks of absence between us.

All that bullshit about being apart making the heart grow fonder or believing that *playing it mean keeps them keen* was just that—utter bullshit. All it did was fester the sort of obsession I wasn't sure anyone could handle.

Except...maybe her.

Tonight, we'd both find out.

Dammit, I should have gone to her. I knew I should have. But I'd hidden in classes, inside the cage, and stayed away because that's what I told myself that she wanted. Because I was as petty as her, and I wanted her to hurt, too.

Fuck, maybe I was human after all.

She wanted to see me in my natural state? Well, here I stood. Everything raw, exposed down to the bone. Filthy, and covered with the blood I'd drawn from other men. Hell, I didn't even know how many.

"No, I wasn't angry at you. Not really. But... missing you hurt. Here." She pressed her palm over her heart. "I didn't know how much it would burn."

"But you *hate me*, remember?" I snarled, stalking toward her. She didn't back away or flinch when I braced both of my arms over her head against the fight club's filthy exoskeleton, the roughened surface covered in graffiti and fuck knew what. "There are marriages that last less time than we've been together in this farce of a fuck buddy relationship. Couples who are public, who kiss and fuck less than we do. My world has been full of you for the better part of two years and then plus some. Only you. I can't do one night a week any more. I need more." I leaned into her space, stealing her breath by design. My design. "And no other man will ever touch you while you're with me. I promise you." I flicked my tongue across her bottom lip, tasting the sweetness of her treat.

"More?" She tried for cavalier and missed the mark by a fucking mile as she tugged the candy out of her mouth and stared up at me with wide eyes. "I couldn't breathe when I was in your room, Dex. I was suffocating," she whispered.

Her panic hovered right beneath the surface of her badass girl persona and I loved both sides of her. My arms ached to fold around her, but that wasn't what either of us needed right now. She might think so, but we'd tried this and it didn't end well.

Eyes full of need and fear and shadows I wanted to kiss away until she softened in my arms then fuck us both into any version of oblivion where she was mine forever watched me. Zin was much more than an obsession.

I needed to wake up tomorrow still wrapped around her for the first time, and give her the world.

Such a fucking perfect temptation.

Closing the final breath between us, I slashed my tongue across her lips in full, licking the sweet taste from her sinful mouth. "So much fucking more."

"Dex—" she whimpered, her sugar-glossed lips parting.

To protest or beg—I didn't care much either way. I took her invitation to let me in the moment her mouth opened, bruising her lips while I explored her with a dormant hunger I rarely acted on but that always lay beneath our playfulness.

My cock thickened as I unleashed the need I quelled for so long, unwilling to keep up the happy-go-lucky Dex façade to play along with her rules and her games.

Fuck the peace. This girl is mine.

My tongue sliced across hers, my brutal kiss driven by pure obsession, my heart drunk on the taste of her. Fuck, we hadn't started yet and already I was intoxicated, addicted to her with a single kiss and craving more. I dropped one hand to cup her ass and pin her against my body until we were both panting and moaning into each other's mouths.

Not a single word of protest left her lips when I drew back for breath, nor did her hands already tangled in my tee push me away.

My heart pounded its victory lap, but my eyes were only for her.

"I want you. Here, in my bed. Fuck, anywhere. Everywhere." My voice deepened into the sort of growl I knew did it for her on demand.

Goosebumps erupted along every inch of her exposed flesh, and there was plenty of that in sight thanks to that flimsy as fuck little top she wore. She gripped me tight, her nails digging half-moon ruts into my skin as she trembled from her lips to her thighs. Her pants came fast, almost panicked.

"I don't care if you hurt me," I murmured. Another addiction we could talk about on a different night. "The sort of pain you give me is what I need to fuck you harder." When my usual dirty talk didn't work to soothe her anxiety, I stared into her eyes, seeking answers.

She gave me plenty. All that I needed and more. But reading her stunning eyes wasn't enough. I needed her words. Offering her a sliver of mercy, I eased back an extra breath, recalling her plea that I suffocated her, and waited.

"I'm scared." She shook in my hold but didn't pull away like the last time I reached for her.

I watched her carefully. "Of me?"

"No, never you." Black silken locks dashed across her face, tangling around her pale throat like a collar. I looped my finger through a strand and tugged gently. "I'm not scared of you, Dex."

I raised an eyebrow as I spoke against her kiss-swollen lips. "You were here tonight. You saw what I'm capable of, the worst of me." *I wasn't going to stop until Jericho hauled me off.*

The unspoken message flicked between us, and she nodded, sending one of her own.

You see everything I want you to see.

But Zin wasn't the only one scared of rejection.

"Yes." Her pupils blown wide, she held my gaze and sucked in her bottom lip. I followed the motion, if with my eyes alone for the moment. I'd follow up with my tongue the moment we were done talking. "I'm scared to go there with you, to find out who we could be together. You're right—I've seen friends destroyed by relationships and heartbreak like that is more than I can bear. I've been hurt before, so bad." Her voice shattered a little at the end, taking a sliver of my heart with her because I *knew* what she'd suffered, even now when she still hid behind the stories of others. "I see the pain in– in– those around us when they fall apart. I'm scared to risk that again on my own," she whispered that last admission on a single breath, as though just discovering it herself.

I leaned closer on my fists, my knuckles pressed to the wall, pinning her there like a black butterfly dazed under the spotlight. "You'll never be alone. Anything you risk, we do it together. And I'll be the first to break if we stop now, Zin. What we have—it's been more than good sex for years. I fucking love you, and I won't stop. You're so much more than just a fuck buddy to me. I don't want to let you go." I didn't give her a chance to answer before I slammed my mouth over hers in a dominating kiss she returned breathlessly.

"Don't go. Please. I don't want to be without you."

It was all I needed to hear. She hadn't said she didn't want to be alone—she said she didn't want to be *without me.*

My heart thundered inside my chest, the too-close cavity crushing the swelling organ so tight I could barely breathe. "You're beautiful," I rasped.

"So are you," she whispered back, light fingertips trailing through the grit and blood that coated me.

I claimed her mouth again, and neither of us spoke. Desperate sounds tore from her throat and I swallowed them all. Sliding both hands down to her ass, I flicked up her flimsy little skirt to cup her perfect globes. A single thin, silky strand slid between them. *My girl came prepared.* I traced my finger over her heat and back to her ass, pressing in enough to earn a feral moan from her.

"Fuck me. You come here of all places and dress like this? You look like motherfucking bait."

"Only you. I dress like this only for you," she whispered, latching her hands around my shoulders beneath my soaking shirt to claw at my salty skin with her nails. When she raised her gaze to mine, diamond drops framed her thick lashes.

She fucking loves me.

I ground my groin into her soft body, hooking her knees over my hips and pushed her thong aside. She dripped on my fingers as I freed my cock into my fist and slammed raw and deep on the first thrust. Her welcoming pussy strangled my cock, tight and slick and hot as I plunged into her.

Zin screamed into my mouth, lost in the moment, desperate and writhing in my arms.

"I love you," I growled, pistioning my hips into her searing heat.

Nothing was fast enough to take the edge off my need as I pummeled her into the side of the building.

"*Dex,*" she cried out, her liquid walls already tightening around my cock.

The fight hadn't worked. I couldn't thrash her out of my system, but I sure as fuck could burn her into my soul. Zin writhed, pinned on my cock where I had a front row seat to every inch of her pulsing arousal.

"If we do this again, if I come back—I don't leave. You stay with me. I stay with you. We wake up in the morning together, every damn sunrise. I'm never leaving your fucking room to walk across campus in the middle of the night nursing an aching heart ever again. Do you understand me?"

"I just want you." She nodded, her words and pleas an insensible mix as she gushed hot and fresh on my cock. Her lashes fluttered as I drove into her faster.

"Just me?" I teased, my voice gravelly.

"Shut up and fuck me, Dex." She rolled her hips, pulsing around my cock with the beginnings of her pleasure.

"You come for me and only me from right now," I grated. "We do this the right way. You've got my heart, Zin. I'm yours. Always."

Her cry ripped free as she milked me, root to tip. "Yes! I love you, I want you—"

Clawed hands contracted on my shoulders at the same time as her pussy strangled my cock, marking me. I threw my head back, shouting my own release to the night. I didn't care who heard us. My only thoughts were for the stunning woman in my arms.

"I love you," I whispered, bracing my arms against the wall behind her back so the brick wouldn't graze her tender skin, remaining lodged balls deep in her and unwilling to move.

She nodded, weary but sated. Her lips pressed to my neck where I thought she might have bitten me. It didn't matter. Cool night air traced my scorched skin. I knew I had to move though I could have stayed buried in her all fucking night and do it all again later. A pained whimper fell from her lips as I shifted.

"Take it easy, Zin." I withdrew from the hot, soaked sheath of her, careful of her tender, bruised skin, placing her feet back on the ground and holding her up when her legs failed. Tucking my cock away, I used the hem of my shirt to wipe her swollen skin where I'd slammed into her on repeat. I didn't have much to clean her up with, and she'd be dripping with my cum as we walked back to campus. "You have my heart. Always. From our first time. Hell, since the first day I saw you."

I stroked her hair as she mumbled something into my shirt that I couldn't make out. Tucking my knuckles beneath her chin, I tilted her head back. Dark shadows of mascara tracked her cheeks. Lip gloss smeared across the corners of her mouth where I hadn't eaten it away. Her eyes glistened with fear and love and everything in between. She had never looked so fucking beautiful.

"I've got you." I nudged her nose with mine and kissed her softly while she murmured something I couldn't hear against my lips. "Say that again, Zinzi."

"I love you. And I've got you, too." She lifted her head as though parting from my skin was the hardest thing she could do right now and smiled. "I tried to hate you so I couldn't feel anything, but not letting you in just made it worse."

My own craving was reflected in her dozy, sated eyes. I crushed her against me where she fit into every hollow of my body the way she always had.

Perfect, beautiful, and mine.

Just mine.

CHAPTER TWELVE

ZINZI

Dex woke me with a mind blowing morning orgasm. I loved it. And that was the problem. Because I wasn't sure what I loved more—his orgasms, or him. Not that it mattered right now. Because my legs already trembled from the eight mile walk from the place where he'd been fighting all the way back to campus after a rough round with him.

He'd showered both of us, and I'd been asleep in his arms before our bodies hit his mattress mere minutes after we entered his bedroom, but at least we were clean.

And he'd left his bedroom window open before we entered, as though he knew—or maybe he hoped

—that he would return with me tonight. Or one night.

The hope was the part that got me. And maybe the fact that I woke up with his tongue doing magic things between my legs. His fingers banded around my wrists where he held them firmly over my stomach—enough that I could pull free, maybe—if I chose, but...

I didn't. Pull away, that was. I stayed right where he wanted me.

I bit my lip to hold my moans in, my thighs trembling over his shoulders as I gushed on his tongue mere moments after I woke.

"Fuck," I breathed, letting my legs fall open as he slithered his way up my body to lodge himself deep inside me. One hand found my hip, the other tangled in my hair.

"Taste yourself on my tongue, sweetness," he murmured, staring down at me before he leaned in and offered me his mouth.

I let my eyes fall shut, opening my lips to lick his tongue with mine as he glided his thick cock in and out of me. The choked cry that tore from me at the overstimulated feeling, my body still pulsing from my last orgasm, drew a dark laugh from him.

"More, please," I whimpered, tilting my hips up

to meet him. Or at least I tried to, but his hand was in the road. I stared up at him, confused. "Dex?"

"You want more, sweetness?" he murmured, grazing my mouth with his, then deepened the kiss until I moaned. "We're taking it slow today."

"Slow?" My brain refused to kick in. I wrapped my legs around his hips and he let me, digging my heels into his ass. "Deeper," I begged, pleading with him.

"Already?" He brushed hair back from my temple with his thumb. "Sweetness, we have a long way to go if you think you're begging already." He kissed me again—mostly to shut me up, I suspected —as the horror that he wasn't, in fact, going to fuck me into oblivion as always advertised with Dex.

Nope, this morning he seemed determined to make love to me.

My trembling legs would bever forgive him, and after I sweated my way through who knew how many orgasms, my voice already raw, my body aching all over and filled with pleasure as he watched my face without reprieve, I decided that neither would I.

And every time I begged him to fuck me harder, he kissed me with a tender touch and drove his cock deeper, triggering another orgasm until I was an overstimulated hot, shivering mess beneath him on his bed.

I had no idea how long his body glided over mine for, but at the end, when he dug his fingers into my hip and kissed me impossibly deeper than before, staring into my eyes as he filled me with his seed, I knew I had been underestimating Dex Breaker's stamina for years.

He held me afterward, letting us roll onto our sides as he stroked his fingers along my body, tucking me into his chest. I rested my head against the smattering of dark curls over his pecs, playing with the fine hairs.

"Dex," I murmured, licking a drop of salt from his skin as he groaned, cupping his rough hand behind my head to hold me against him. "You got new ink."

He laughed. "Not recently, sweetness."

I caught his hand, the one he had broken, and pulled it from over my shoulder to study the still fresh black ink on his wrist. "This. It was under your cast when the doctor took it off. I remember seeing it. And I remember it not being there before."

"You know me that well, huh?" He laughed down at me.

I didn't. "Yeah. I do."

His smile faded as I played, tracing the lines I now identified as a thick black band that was heavier halfway up his arm that faded toward his hand. Several flowerlike patterns were etched into it, but I couldn't figure out how it was done.

"It's white ink over black,' he said quietly. "I got sick of feeling the pain from the break, so I had something else done to distract me. It's an addiction, of sorts. Like you."

"I'm your addiction? That doesn't sound healthy."

I let him tuck me back into his chest and entertained myself by trailing my hands up and down his hard, washboard abs. Dex's body went well beyond the usual six or eight-pack. He barely had an inch of excess anything on him, unless it was pure muscle. Maybe a few tendons.

And a whole lot of ink.

"It's not healthy. But I'm still not letting you go. And I want to make you breakfast."

I rubbed my cheek against his chest. "You need to know something about me."

"I know."

"No, I mean, here." I grabbed his hand and pulled it lower, to my stomach where my skin looked fine except for a pale slice, but the scar tissue beneath told a different story.

"I know."

"No, you don't. I haven't told you." I frowned up at him.

"I searched for you." His head tipped to one side as he looked down at me, propping one hand behind his head. "*We* searched for you. A long time ago. To make sure you were safe. When you have a mafia and billionaire lord housemate, these things are... normal. Or, not normal. We did the same with Bella and Rose more recently. When Nelson finds his significant other, then we will do the same for them."

I stared up at him, my stomach cramping, though I wasn't due for a few more weeks. "All this time?" He'd known my history, everything I'd suffered...and he hadn't mentioned it? Not once?

He nodded. "Yeah. It's okay, Zin. And he won't touch you once he's out. I promise you."

I scrambled backward until my butt hit the wall. "No. No, you shouldn't have—"

"Told you before now?" Dex rolled with me, pining me beneath him. "Told you that I looked you up two and a half years ago, found out the man who stabbed the fuck out of you is in jail, that you got yourself fixed up—alone, because there's no family for you to rely on—and that scared the shit out of you? Rightfully so." He never looked away, never once flinched despite my heart hammering at his chest. "Did you think I wouldn't get it that someone hurt you and that you didn't want to talk about it, Zin? I knew there was something. I never wanted to push you. I just wanted to make sure you were safe." He leaned down, and kissed me.

We both tasted my tears. My broken trust.

"You should have told me," I whispered.

"To what end?" He shrugged. "If he got out before we got to this point, Falcon and I would have dealt with it. He's not your problem anymore, Zin."

I stared at him, the suffocating feeling descending on me in this same black painted room once again. If I hadn't been lying down, I would have fallen. There was no denying what he meant.

"I can't accept—" I choked.

His thumb grazed my temple. "You don't have to," he murmured. "I'll look after you, Zin. I always have."

I blinked at him, then shoved at his chest. "No."

"No?" He crouched back on his haunches, an almost comical look on his face. "I give you unlimited orgasms, and you tell me no?"

"Orgasms are not bargaining chips," I told him as I threw my clothes on, finding what I could from the night before. My thong was absent so I forewent that, and headed for his door.

"I mean, they could be." He grabbed a pair of sweats and donned them in record time, then pulled me into his arms. "Slow down. Breakfast, remember? You're staying. We don't run, not anymore."

I bit my lip. "You said you look after me, right?"

"Yeah." His gaze darkened, hooded and heavy as he cupped my cheek and leaned in to kiss me.

A good thing, because I didn't have the energy or the volume to yell this next bit at him. "The fights with Beau?" He stopped. "The group session with Falcon and Nelson who just appeared in my class?"

Dex stilled, his lips a breath from mine, and said nothing.

Tears sheened my vision with a curtain of salt as I gently detached myself from his hold. "I might love you, and you might think you love me, Dex Breaker," I whispered, "but we are toxic as all hell for each other. And nothing we do seems to be able to stop that."

"Zin," he growled, linking an arm around my waist to pull me in.

This time I was ready for him. I grabbed for the

door handle to his room, pirouetting on trembling legs that thankfully worked on demand, and twisted in the other direction out of his hold.

"Bye, Dex," I whispered, and shut the door between us.

"Zin?" Nelson sat at the kitchen table looking the worse for wear with an askew bow tie and a towel wrapped loosely around his waist. "I didn't know you were here."

"I'm leaving." I walked across to him and pressed a kiss to the top of his head just as the door to Dex's room opened.

Nelson stiffened. "She instigated the contact. I did not."

"It's fine." Dex waved a hand. "Zin. Please?"

I shook my head, willing the tears to stay inside for just a little longer. "Not this time, Dex. It's not for us."

He nodded. "You want me to come find you later? Make sure you're okay?"

My heart ached at the emotion thickening his voice. "No."

Nelson grabbed my hand. "Whatever he did, he didn't mean it."

"You're a sweetie. But you shouldn't have checked up on me."

His face fell. "Oh."

I nodded. "Oh." My vision blurred again. "Bye, Nelson."

Neither of them stopped me as I walked out of their dorm room and headed down the stairs.

And right into the arms of a pair of identical twins with unsmiling faces.

CHAPTER THIRTEEN

DEX

"You let her go?" Falcon snarled in my face. Bella made soft sounds of protest at his side, but he pushed her back into Rose's arms. "Bedroom. Keep her occupied. *Now*, Rose," he growled.

Rose made an uncomfortable, but very Italian noise and towed a protesting Bella away, gesturing frantically to me behind Falcon's back.

I didn't speak finger Italian or mafia talk, but I figured that was hand language for *fix this shit right now or so help me God*.

"She didn't want to stay, Falcon. What was I supposed to do, tie her to the bed?"

Both Nelson and Falcon paused for a moment, considering the options.

I barked a laugh. "Let's consider the legal ramifications of that statement before you answer, and what just got us in shit with her."

"Mafia." Falcon raised the gun usually attached to him at some point.

"Lord." Nelson hefted the wallet that had gotten him out of more than a few scrapes, most on the other side of legal.

I glared at both of them. "We do not keep women who don't want to be here because we want them more than they do."

In Falcon's bedroom, Bella moaned loudly.

Falcon smirked. "Case in point?"

I glowered at him. "Not what I meant."

"Isn't it?" He sauntered forward. "Maybe she needs more orgasms. A pleasured woman is a happy woman."

"She had plenty of orgasms, thank you," I spat.

"She was still walking."

I closed my eyes. "You're missing the fucking point. She left because we broke her rules."

"She should be playing by yours."

I turned my back on Falcon, willing myself not to slam my fist in his face and break my other pinky. By the time I hit *four* in my reverse count from ten back to one, my breathing had evened. I turned back around.

"Zin wanted to tell me her secrets. She didn't want to know that we had snooped on her and found out on our own."

"You are a bit shit at keeping secrets," Nelson put in.

I ground my teeth. "Not. The. Fucking. Point."

Bella moaned again.

Falcon smiled, leaning back against the wall to scratch his shoulder blades. "The perfect soundtrack."

"Doesn't it bother you, him giving her that much pleasure?" I changed tack. "What if she falls for him, instead of you?"

Falcon laughed at me. "Are you that insecure? We love—" he paused to draw a sloppy air triangle, "— each other. Not once would they cheat on me, nor me on them. That's the sort of loyalty you can't buy, Dex. I give them parts of me that no one else gets. My love. My secrets. My heart. In return, they offer me theirs. I keep that safe and protect them. Yes, even if it means from themselves. Right now, Rose can't be in this conversation because he'd probably try to kill you. Bella would cry and try to save everyone. Or maybe it would be a bloodbath. I haven't quite worked my little brat out yet." He smiled. "But when I go back in there, he'll pull his cock out of her ass, hold her open for me, and kiss her while I screw them both into the floor until it shakes. What part of that is missing between you and Zin?"

I stared at him and swallowed. "The part where I let her leave because she's fucking miserable with me."

"No, my friend." He reached across and squeezed my shoulder hard enough to hurt. "You let her go because you were scared of hurting her more. She left because she's scared of being compressed. But there is no place safer for her than with you, and she is happier with you than she is any other time."

A lump lodged in my throat. "And you fucking well know this how, you little stalker?" I snapped, hating how right he sounded, how logical, when my brain told me to let her go and let her make her own decisions.

"Because she came to you last night on her own."

I stared at him.

Nelson cheered.

"Go find her. I have a brat to fuck. I suggest you leave, too." Falcon cast a spare glance at Nelson. "It will get loud in here soon."

"And I'm out." Nelson darted into his room, the towel dangling off the end of his hard on, baring his pasty buttocks for the room to see.

Falcon snorted, while I covered my eyes. "Ahh, fine. You've convinced me."

"Good. She won't have gone far." He nodded, a pleased smile on his face.

I watched him, my heart clenching. "Are you like him?" I asked softly.

"Who?" Falcon turned back to me, his hands drifting to his phone.

"Your father."

He stilled. "More than I would like."

I nodded. "Mine didn't remember my name. She doesn't know hers. Consider yourself lucky you have family at all."

He nodded, bowing his head over his phone at the same time as all three of ours lit up.

I frowned, grabbing mine off the edge of the sofa where I'd left the device when I followed Zon out of my room. The picture that came up made no sense at all at first as I struggled to comprehend what I saw.

"*Dex,*" Nelson bellowed, charging naked and still pasty as fuck from his room as it finally clicked in what I was seeing.

Zin, with a twin standing over her, one with his pale hand extended around her throat, the other kneeling with his head positioned between her spread legs where she was tied between them, her mouth held open, eyes wide and terrified.

Falcon knocked my hand away, breaking the hideous vision. "It's not real."

"What?" I stared up at him, but all I could see was the head bent between her open legs.

His hand connected sharply with my cheek, the pain waking me up. "It's not real. I promise you. They've pinned her somewhere, set up the angle, and he's inches from her. He hasn't fucking touched her."

"You know that how?" I stared desperately into my housemate's tense face.

Falcon held my gaze, not once flinching from whatever he read in my expression—the worry, the fear, the anger.

"Because they know you'll kill them if they do."

"The fuck is this." I threw the picture under Beau's nose. "We were done."

He shrugged. "Were we? I don't remember negotiating those terms."

Falcon made one of those Italian noises Rose was so fond of at my back from where he leaned against the entrance to the formal dining room in the Kingsman house. "Start remembering. Otherwise you'll have a new exit hole in the back of your head." He loaded his handgun in front of Beau, ignoring the two other Kingsman frat boys who also drew similar weapons.

"You won't get a shot off," Beau said quietly, his head tipped to one side.

Falcon stopped what he was doing to look straight at Beau. "Do you trust their aim? Because I will not miss."

Beau inclined his head, and the Kingsman boys lowered their guns, though I noted they didn't put them away. I felt distinctly underdressed without one but I'd also been sans location for Zin when I left our dorm and Beau was the first person I thought of with additional resources before I called in my own mini army.

"I remember you saying you'd throw fights for me," Beau said in his hoity as fuck voice.

I smiled, with teeth. "I remember an expiry date of ten weeks. We passed that while I was off with cracked ribs thanks to one of your opponents. You didn't set that caveat, and so we are clean. Would you like a visual reminder? We have video evidence and backup," I added quietly.

Beau watched me. "Cute," he remarked and picked up the glass of cognac he'd been drinking when we first invaded his lair. "The twins don't answer to me. You'd be better off heading to their home and seeing if they're there."

A growl built in my throat, but a tap at my heel from Falcon shut me up. This was the shit he was good at. I had zero patience for Beau's posturing.

"Sure. We could do that. Or we could take something of yours with us as a trade. Say..." Falcon made a show of looking around. "Sylvie?"

Beau flinched. "If you touch her—"

"I'll what, kill you?" I used air quotes because I knew it would piss him off further. "Motherfucker, I'm already there. So let's find my girl and you can have yours back."

A muscle twitched in Beau's jaw. He flipped his phone and pressed call.

I waited.

Falcon cleaned his gun.

And on the other end of Beau's girlfriend's line,

Nelson picked up. His British accent came through loud and clear.

"Hello there, my boy. I have something of yours."

"You have a short fucking lifespan, is what you have," Beau growled.

"Now, let's be nice. Sylvie, say hello to your lord and master," Nelson prompted.

"Hello, Nelson," I could *hear* the eye roll in her voice, but also the laughter.

"She's in no danger," Falcon said softly. "Where are you, Sylvie?"

"At Madame Kernester's Teahouse, about six blocks from campus. Don't come and get me, Beau. I'm fine. Do what you have to. But we are coming back, and we are getting a tea collection. Maybe some teapots."

Beau glared daggers at me. "We are not getting a teapot collection."

"Oh that one is pretty, Nelson. Yes, please," Sylvie gushed.

I couldn't tell if she was genuinely excited or if she was playing it up, but watching Beau turn purple was fun, personally.

"I'd say your girl doesn't get spoiled often enough if a Lord of Nothingness can make her day. Right, pet?" I swore Nelson tweaked her nose.

It seemed like everyone else in the room heard the contact in his voice too.

"Don't fucking touch her," Beau snapped.

"It's fine, Beau. I'm fine. Nelson might be a bit broke after this shopping trip, but it's fine."

"Not likely, pet."

"She used the f word," I muttered.

"I'll find a word to use for you." Beau's glare shifted to me.

I offered him a shit eating grin, imagining it wasn't often that he met more than one person who outclassed him on the financial front, and in this room he had two, if Nelson counted alongside Falcon. Not everyone wore their wealth in obsequious fashion the way he did.

"Now, tell me where we will find the twins."

CHAPTER FOURTEEN

ZINZI

Darkness eked into every part of my soul. I'd never be able to lie in Dex's darkened bedroom with the drapes closed in full ever again.

That was, assuming I got out of this place with its close walls, and unbreathable air.

My assessment that first day in Dex's black painted room had been right. I was claustrophobic. I had no idea if it was a late onset or if I'd always been like this and was just figuring it out. But right now ruminating on that little stupid and useless piece of trivia was so much better than dealing with the two monsters who shared my space.

Both had pale eyes tinged with red rings, pale skin and identical features. Pale hair, so light it was almost colorless or gray in this unfathomable light. Their bodies were like ghosts or worms in the void that surrounded us that could have gone on and on... or walls that shifted, containing me until they were right there and all I had was a handful of breaths before my last remaining breath of air ran out.

It was enough to make me want to scream, so that was what I did.

Scream and scream and scream, shaking my arms locked in their metal shackles they had screwed to my wrists and ankles when they perched me on my box and pinned me in place and took those fucking pictures that were almost as hideous as them.

And then they turned out the lights, and the all-pervading darkness made it so much worse. Because then my mind wandered and I lost track of time and place and how much space there was between me and them.

All I could hear was my breathing, and them. The screams were preferable, and so I did that instead.

Until I couldn't scream anymore.

Then my head hung between my shoulders and I panted, my throat raw, my body sweat sheened and cold and exhausted.

Which was when they began to talk, their conversation bouncing off one another like they were two versions of the same person, only not.

"Strange, isn't it?"

"Very strange."

"To make such noise."

"I didn't think it would go so long."

"The last one who screamed like that—

"—we ended before it stopped."

"But that just kept going and going and going."

"Like it would never stop."

Their words bounced back and forth, my head turning in the darkness, seeking them out. The slivers of light when they shifted, gifting me horrific glimpses of too gaunt faces, pale hair, and red eyes. Skin that looked like it had been interred for months, not of the living at all.

And their words—

Almost poetic, their phrases ran with a sort of cadence I barely understood but did all the same.

Because this was Key and Kash Laurent. The hellish twins of Rippton U. If all the rumors I never listened to held true, they were psychopaths who murdered for money, favors and fun.

I believed every single myth about them right now in this place.

"You're insane," I whispered. "Both of you." I hadn't convinced myself that I wasn't hallucinating, and they were just one person my demented, terrified mind had split into two.

"Which one does she mean?"

"You?"

"Or me?"

"It can only be one of us."

"But then she must be lying."

"Because she means both of us."

Twin, matching grins met me at too close a range. I shrank back against nothing but air behind me and nearly fell off the harsh wooden box I was seated on. The chains holding my wrists in their shackles jangled against the floor as I struggled to stay upright.

Suddenly that was important. I didn't want my face near the ground. Once I was down there, I doubted they would let me up and then there was nothing but...

Pain.

An old friend, and one I didn't want to revisit today.

"He'll come," I whispered the promise to myself.

Of course, the freaky as fuck twins chimed in.

"Yes he will."

"Of course he will."

"That is the point, after all."

"For him to come, and you to die."

"For him. So he knows."

"That he cannot break the rules."

Rules. That's what started all of this.. Me and my stupid, fucking rules. Tears flowed along my cheeks as I bowed my head and said a different prayer than anyone I ever hoped I would ever say.

Dex, don't find me. Nelson, don't help him. Falcon, forget I exist. Please.

Then they'd all be safe.

A twin brushed my cheek with deathly cold fingers. "Such pretty tracks. More, please," he whispered, licking the tips of his fingers and touching them to his lips. "Despair tastes sweetest from the source."

My woeful prayer said to the shadows, my voice a mere rasp, I let my tears run and run and run.

I cracked dry eyes open to find a man sharing my box, holding a condensing glass of water in a proffered, manicured hand. It took me a few blinks, but we got there. Or at least, I did.

"You're Beau Bennett."

"Yes, ma'am." He held the glass steady.

Eventually I took it, realizing that I didn't shake or jangle any more. And that I could see. The room seemed bigger, and the horrifying twins weren't present.

But the door was still shut and, I guessed, locked.

Still, I felt safer with this man than the ones before, so that was something.

"What changed?"

"Dex Breaker changed. And Falcon Gianio, and Nelson Milton. Actually, I'll probably have to offer them places in the Kingsman frat after this." He rubbed at the back of his neck and looked amused.

"They aren't dead?" I screeched and flung myself out at him, only to find my body held at arm's length.

"I prefer hygienic females, and since mine is currently a hostage, I thought we should negotiate terms of release," he said in a soft, respectful tone, considering his words.

"You...are negotiating, with me?" I pushed the rest of his words aside. "Why?"

"Falcon mentioned a marketing pack for the frat. If you would?" Beau motioned to the water and raised an eyebrow.

"Falcon..?" I blinked, gulped the rest of my water,

and my brain ticked over. "The branding pack. Oh, Beau. That frazzled lion has got to go. Here's what we planned."

He listened to me talk in my ruined voice for what had to be half an hour, but I wasn't wasting my chance to get in front of the rumored head of the Kingsman frat when I'd been working on that fucking group project for weeks—months—with Falcon and Nelson. Both who, admittedly, have excellent brains and also took direction well.

He waited until I finished. "We?"

I nodded. "Nelson, Falcon and myself have been working on this together this semester. I can produce the entire media kit for you...if I can leave the room. There's other strategy bits..." I shrugged.

Beau rolled his lips. "Can you pitch me off the top of your head?"

"Can I? Beau Bennett. I'm a marketing student. Don't offend me."

He smiled. "The floor is yours."

I talked until my already raw voice ran dry, and he listened. Actually listened, not pretended. A few interjected questions and I swore we were there. His phone buzzed a half second before the door crashed inward and my dusty, dirty saviors arrived.

"Bravo. You found us before the air ran out."

Beau cocked his head to one side as he considered Dex, Nelson and Falcon, who stared around the small, brightly lit space with confusion. "Or was she ever in any danger at all?"

Dex looked at me. "Zin?"

I glanced at Beau who actually twiddled his thumbs and attempted to look innocent.

Good fucking luck with that.

"I was, but I believe we are good now. Or was that simply a distraction?" I raised my eyebrows at Beau, unimpressed if the latter was true.

He shook his head. "I agree with your assessment and the three of you are hired. Change the branding up. Also, you three have rooms. Barclay is moving in with a few friends, and I have space to fill. From what I've heard, you've been living in shithouse dorms. There's room for extras," he nodded to me though I didn't appreciate coming under the heading of an 'extra', "and I'll find you a better space to fight in. Deal?"

Dex folded his arms. "You're out of your fucking—"

I body slammed him by accident. Okay, half by accident. "Deal," I said into his shirt for him. "Nelson needs a home. He won't survive without you two."

Falcon laughed. "She's right. You want to tell

her?"

I looked between him and Dex. "Tell me what?"

Nelson gave me puppy eyes. "Your friend is the reason I have this." He pulled his shirt up to expose a long, pink scar. "Twins, on his orders."

I glared at Beau over my shoulder. "Deal rescinded."

"Not rescinded," Falcon said lazily. "We need a different presence in the Kingsman frat. Who knows? Maybe there's new leadership required."

Beau held his gaze. "Don't bet on it."

Dex's arms tightened around me. "You're okay? Gonna tell me what happened?"

I swallowed as the first hours...day?...slammed back into me. I swayed into him. "Later, is that okay?" I whispered.

He nodded. "All the time in the world, sweetness. Tell me when you're ready."

I nuzzled into his chest and sighed. For the first time in hours, I sucked in a full breath.

We were going to be fine.

CHAPTER FIFTEEN

DEX

The Kingsman frat boasted a new logo and merch in their campus and online shop in short order. Once Zinzi started, she was a whirlwind powerhouse that was a genuine joy to watch. Falcon and Nelson, however, had the dubious joy of working with her. Dubious, because they had to keep up and neither of them did so well on lack of sleep or being told what to do around the clock.

Beau seemed to find the whole thing hilarious and was a lot more personable with Sylvie back by his side, though thanks to Nelson's delivery service and gifts to his girlfriend, he now also was the unhappy owner of a teapot wall that Sylvie had installed in his bedroom.

"You're happy?" I asked Zin, lifting her hair to press a line of kisses along her shoulders where she worked on her laptop in a nightie, perched on my bed, sharing my desk space. I still had a lot of work to catch up with from being off with broken bits and chasing a wounded heart, but having her with me helped. A whole hell of a lot.

"Happy?" She raised a glowing face to mine for a kiss I happily provided. "Are you kidding? Beau throws me challenges at every turn. I love it. It's like fighting with someone who actually has a brain. Not that you don't have a brain, but he is...aggressive. I enjoy the challenge."

"You enjoy working and having something to do." I kissed the top of her head.

"Yep."

"Good. As long as he doesn't take all your time up." I lifted her body and slipped beneath her so she straddled my lap. "Because I still need time with my girl."

"Not right now." She wiggled her ass temptingly in my lap.

"Nope." I kissed the top of her head, then the corner of her mouth as she frowned. "For luck?"

"Why do you need luck?" Her attention successfully severed from her laptop, she tipped her mouth back, seeking mine. "What are you doing?"

I kissed her back, threading my hands through hair and made it deep and long until her whole body softened on my lap. "That's what I was after, sweetness. I'm fighting Beau."

"What? Now?" she shrieked in my ear. "Are you fucking insane?"

I shrugged. "Jury's out. I'm probably deaf after that, but who really knows. It's safe, Zin."

"Safe, my ass. He held me in a locked room until you got there."

"Without the twins."

She glared at me. "They told me you were going to die."

My hand curved around her face. "Didn't happen, Zin. Won't happen today, either." I hoped. Because if I passed Beau's little test then we had an extra side deal I needed him for, very soon. "No blades. No weapons. Just our hands and feet."

She gritted her teeth. "It's Beau Bennett. If it was anyone else I wouldn't be worried."

"Aw, you're worried? You are a sweetie."

She batted my hand away. "Fuck you, Dex," she huffed.

"Later, sweetness. Save some energy for me. Because I want you to drench this bed when I fuck you tonight." I kissed her again until she was breathless, massaging her nape, then I let her go and slipped out the door before she could argue.

And no way in hell did I want her anywhere near the impromptu fight ring in that scant little nightie that I loved on her. The frat boys were horndogs and my girl was mine. Falcon might be all for sharing, but I didn't have those proclivities. My girl was mine alone, and I needed to get this fight done so Beau held up his end of the bargain.

Because his connections could get us where Nelson, Falcon and I fell short.

That I needed his help irritated the shit out of me. But being able to bang it out together—albeit at each other—evened the field somewhat. Plus, I was interested to see if the man was as brutal as myths surrounding him suggested.

The grassed area out the back of the frat house had been cleared of furniture, and a rope pulled about in a circular shape. I knew Zin would be able to see us from my window so I gave her a little wave as I walked backwards out of the house that she didn't return, but she did plant her elbows on the windowsill, and didn't move.

I sighed. So much for her being distracted with work while Beau and I beat the shit out of each other.

I found Falcon nearby, holding wrapping in his hands. I shook my head. "Never used it in the ring. Not about to start."

"And if he uses glass?"

"Then he'll have a short fall to the dirt and a brutal ending."

I wasn't about to pull my punches with this one. The deal was no weapons of any sort. I wasn't in for cheating and I'd made that abundantly clear. I also made it clear that if I found out Beau took assistance, I'd be putting him down—in the hospital bed variety.

"Then let's hope to fuck he doesn't cheat, because Nelson's shit in a fight," Falcon muttered. "And there's a whole lot more of them than us."

"This is us, man. We do this right, we have more of us to go around." I held his gaze.

He nodded slowly.

Swell the ranks. That was the whole point of this endeavor. Falcon needed allies away from his father. I needed assistance on a little side job. Nelson needed...well, Nelson needed a lot of things. I wasn't sure what topped the list, but a lifeline came first if he kept flirting with Sylvie and buying Beau's girl-friend teapots.

"Time to go." Nelson skidded to a stop beside me, no teapots in sight, strangling his bowtie, and grinning like a loon.

"What's made you so happy?"

I shoved the second offer of hand wraps away from Falcon.

"I just met the other lord."

"Who?" I raised my head from running through everything I knew about Beau Bennett.

Left handed, vicious bastard, captain of the lacrosse team, aggressor from the get go, likely had a huge depth of stamina. He had a proclivity for BDSM —apparently the pretty Sylvie played up as his sub/brat. Falcon eyed her off one too many times, and the frat head had a word in his ear. He weighed in with less muscle than me, but I wouldn't out last the asshole. Which meant I needed to end this quick, and early.

Nelson drew a deep breath. "Barclay Augusts Chesterfield, famously involved with his French manservant and another female fling at the same time, just asked his crush on a castle date, Earl of—"

"You're up." Falcon tapped me on the shoulder and saved me from what I suspected would be a long winded explanation of a lineage that only one person in the crowd apart from the person who belonged to it cared for.

"I'm happy for you, mate." Nelson's Brit was rubbing off on me.

"Kissy for good luck?" He puckered up on cue.

I face palmed him, shoving him back with a snort. "Thanks for the offer."

I turned away, feeling Falcon's clap against my back but my gaze was on Zinzi where she hadn't moved from my window overlooking the lawn area behind the house. Her gaze locked on mine as I kicked my knuckles and raised them to her. *For you, sweetness.* She didn't know it yet. And she might get pissy with me later, but also I knew she'd understand.

Eventually.

"Ready?"

A different voice broke into my reverie.

I nodded, and turned to face Beau who faced me bare knuckled and bare chested. Lean muscle, ink and scars decorated his chest in a jigsaw that I spent the next thirty minutes studying at various angles, having failed to do what I intended and put him down early. What my opponent lacked in musculature, he made up for in speed, agility and quick thinking.

My respect for him grew through my patience for his games waned.

"I'll be glad to get this done," I said to Falcon on my third and final break. We'd agreed to limited rounds, and the next to fall down, stayed down.

"If it works out in your favor." Falcon doctored the damn cut over my eye that refused to stay shut. Neither my hand nor my ribs played up, though something on Beau cracked with the last blow I landed to his side.

"Thanks for the heads up. I'll remember you for my next positivity Ted X talk." I clasped hands with Falcon and nodded to Nelson who texted quickly from his seated position. I suspected he played both sides of the fence, chatting alternately with Zinzi and Sylvie to keep them in the loop and not worrying.

"Look after the girls," I said quietly. "We'll be done soon."

He nodded, and didn't look up.

I turned back to the temporary ring and walked in, rolling both shoulders and taking stock. No part of me wanted to get cold and while the frat boys might want this event to take all night, I was used to knocking through fights a whole lot faster.

"Come on, old man," I called to a round of ribald cheers.

Beau watched me with a strange smile on his face, and I knew at that moment what the outcome of this round would be before he stepped foot back in our impromptu ring.

Hell, I even started counting out the blows we traded.

He made it look good, that was certain. I didn't know if I had cracked something on him earlier, or if he'd always intended to reciprocate, but just over what should have been halfway through our third round, I swung hard into his jaw in a blow he should have dodged, and he dropped.

Straight to the grass, and stayed there.

"Out cold." Falcon checked Beau, who didn't move. To his credit, his friend, Crush called it the same without any other reaction, like they'd planned it.

"He's done. Your winner." The captain of the ice hockey team held my hand above my head, and I knew he was as full of shit as his friend.

I raised my eyebrows and said nothing as the slightly stunned crowd of loyal Kingsman boys who were well past drunk at this stage. The entire frat watched the unexpected outcome, then broke into cheers, stamping around Beau who was dragged off to the side of the grass and babysat by Crush and Nelson who took up residence on his other side, checking his pulse occasionally and slapping his face lightly until he roused a moment later.

I shook my head as he offered me a sloppy grin for show, taking the bottle of water Crush offered, the two of them speaking softly. Even Nelson had a thing or two to say, and Beau surprised me again when he embraced the young lordling and even straightened his bow tie.

"Beau Bennett threw a fight. Who the fuck knew," Falcon muttered in my ear.

"Keep it down. They seem to have bought that bullshit," I grunted, looking around at the hockey boys who drank and fucking drank until the house ran dry. The lacrosse team might be a different story but maybe they knew their captain better than the rest of the Allstars. I wasn't completely up on the frat house interrelations just yet. Something told me I was about to be.

"That mean he'll help us?"

I shrugged. "Guess we'll find out. We don't seem to be on his shit list anymore."

Who knew about the twins. As long as they stayed the fuck away from my girl, I was good for now.

"Go shower. She's waiting for you." Nelson appeared at my side.

"Are you done hugging the enemy?" Falcon growled.

"Not the enemy. We have a date." He flashed his screen. "So do I. Before my new friend heads off to his castle in France for a quick see-his-evil-step-mother holiday, I have coffee with an Earl." He emitted a high pitched noise.

"Did you just squeeee?" Zin rubbed her eyes, sliding beneath my sweaty arm. "And did Beau really pass out when you bitch slapped him?"

"Yes and no. Let me tell you a story because you sure as fuck should not be down here wearing that." I eyed her in the nightie that should never have left my bedroom, and certainly not with her inside it.

"I wore a robe," she protested, waving to the completely transparent piece of material that only highlighted her curves and drew every eye in the vicinity.

"Too many drunken dicks down here for my liking, sweetness." I kissed her mouth hard, needing her. "Come on. We need to let Nelson fangirl, schedule us in, and I need a shower. Then I have a promise to keep."

I swore she fucking glowed back at me.

"Alright," she whispered, just loud enough for everyone in the vicinity to hear.

Falcon and Nelson both groaned.

"Offer's open to share, my brother." Falcon slapped my back for the last time that night.

I shook my head. "Not my game, my man." I looped an arm around Zin, towing her upstairs. "I'll be a second. Get naked for me?"

She nodded and slipped the gown off her shoulders once we were safely inside my room, dropping the straps for her nightie too. "Hurry?"

I've never showered so damn fast in my life.

The aches earned during my fight with Beau—and all the hits from the first long two rounds that weren't faked whatsoever—could start come morning. Right now, I had a few other things on my mind, starting with one very naked Zinzi in my bed.

I pulled my door open to find her curled completely bare, as requested, in the middle of my bed, the covers pulled back. Her black hair hung straight down her back, and her shoulders arched where she leaned on her hands, her head tilted to one side.

"You weren't too long," Zin murmured.

"I didn't want to leave you waiting." I tossed my towel to the floor and was on the bed in two strides, my arms around her.

She arched when I nuzzled her neck, pressing her pert tits into my chest. I took the hint and dived down, sucking her nipples into my mouth one by one until she moaned and leaned back for me, spreading her legs with my palms and finding her tender places to work open until she gushed hot and ready.

"I fell asleep before. I thought you might be a while," she admitted.

"Did we bore you?" I nipped the side of her breast and she gasped, batting at me.

"Ow," she whispered.

I sucked on the same spot until she whimpered, then pulled back to admire the bruise I'd left. "Too much?"

"No, I just... we never played like that. Before," Zin bit her lip.

I leaned up for a kiss, sucking her lip into my mouth and sliding my tongue deep as she reached for me, fisting my cock and working me hard. My own groan fell from my lips as she smiled into my kiss.

"Fuck, I love you," I muttered.

"I love that I can make you groan like that," she whispered. "And that you get hard from playing with me."

"You're the biggest turn on in my world, baby. Let me mark you up a bit. If you don't mind the pain?" I pulled back to look into her eyes.

She shook her head after a moment. I took it slow, nipping her other breast below her nipple, then sucking lightly at the flesh to ease the pain as I fingered her hard. She came the second time I bit her, mixing pain and pleasure together as I reprogramed her body to like me marking her.

The third time, I worked on the inside of her thigh, and followed up with playing with her perfect pussy. Her thighs wrapped around my head after that, and I stayed there, rewarding her for taking the pain I gave her, licking and touching and teasing until she trembled on my tongue all over again.

And when I thought she'd fall apart from pleasure I forced her to straddle me, holding her up and drove her onto my dick, fucking her hard and fast from below. Her screams redecorated the walls of my new room with their echoes. I leaned back, reveling in the feel of her riding me, the pleasure of her body trembling as she struggled to take me, cumming over again until I let myself fill her and crushed her to my chest, her name written in the last breath that emptied my chest cavity.

And then we slept, our bodies tangled, my dick still lodged inside her hot little body. The girl I thought would break me apart but instead, knotted us closer together.

EPILOGUE ONE

DEX

My borrowed black tactical gear fit like shit and weighed too much but it did the job and got us through the third door of the prison where Ledger Raymond was secured, along with our fake IDs that proclaimed myself, Falcon, Nelson and Beau, and Crush as prison guards for the facility. Not that any of us had an idea what guards should be doing at three in the morning, but it didn't matter.

Right now the screens and cameras recorded exactly nothing because we'd paid for the privilege. The doors opened on demand because we had paid for that too. Beau's promise paid off—so far. I was keen to get this job done and get the fuck out before the time limit on this favor expired and we became permanent residents of the penitentiary.

"One more door." Falcon had memorized the map as well as I had, and we were counting gates as we passed, as well as color coding them in our heads.

"Orange," I muttered.

"You boys are serious," Beau remarked.

"It's a good thing," Crush snapped.

I liked that the Allstars hockey captain wasn't any happier than we were to be here. His friend waited in the car outside. What I didn't like was that we didn't have one of our people with the transport team, but as Nelson kept reminding me, we were all one team now. Tonight was supposed to cement that fact.

"If you say so," Beau murmured.

We'd left the girls back at the frat house, both exhausted after handing in group projects. Which meant that Falcon and Nelson were also exhausted, but they held up. I hoped to fuck they did, or we were two men down.

We passed the orange gate, and Nelson started counting.

"Thirteenth on the right."

"From here?" I clarified, willing myself not to get the wrong door.

"From this door."

"Counting." I marked it out, Ledger Raymond's ugly as fuck face burned into my memory. He'd be a whole less pretty and wouldn't need anything to breathe out of after I was done with him.

We made it to the cell, and I frowned. "Did you already open this door?"

Beau shook his head and glanced at me. "No."

"Fuck," Crush swore, and Falcon wasn't far behind him.

A rumpled pile of orange pajamas was crumpled on the floor at the far end of the cell, the remains of the body housed within them stained with enough blood that it obviously wasn't in any condition to breathe.

"The hell happened here?"

"Back up," Falcon said sharply. "Unless you want to join him." He slid a blade into my hand and nodded forward.

I stared at the blond headed man sitting on the bunk bed and the identical twin who emerged from the shadows on the opposite side of the cell. Both were dressed in white baggy pants and singlets and both were splattered with blood.

"Three guesses on who that belongs to." Nelson looked ready to puke beneath his guard's helmet.

No guesses were necessary. Key—or Kash, I never could tell them apart—rose on long, steady legs.

"We heard you needed a favor."

"We wanted to make up for scaring your girl."

"We believed it was necessary."

"We were wrong."

I blinked. After a day, when she could stomach it, Zinzi had related their odd and terrifying incarceration with her when she was sure she would die at their hands, their strange way of speaking. Now, I understood the rabbit hole-esque feel of her time with the twins, if not a touch of her terror.

"This is your...apology?" I said carefully, straining for understanding.

"Yes." One of the twins smiled, and it was utterly terrifying. Devoid of all emotion, like a void.

"Gotcha." I turned back to my new team. "We do not need to be here anymore." I pointed back the way we came then turned back to the twins and inclined my head because they seemed to like formalities. "Thank you."

The other twin also smiled horrifically, apparently delighted with my response. "You are welcome, Dexter Breaker."

That he knew my full name freaked me the fuck out. I sympathized with how my girl felt, trapped with these assholes in a room for untold hours at a stretch.

"Moving," Nelson muttered, his voice straining.

That the twins had done what we came to do but with apparent ease bothered everyone except perhaps Beau who seemed to understand them the best. We retreated, Falcon and myself counting every single gated door we passed back through and locking it as we went, though I doubted that would contain the twins, or their clean up.

And when we got back to the car unscathed, Beau called the guard house to let them know that we were out, not a single one of us spoke on the trip back to the frat house. I climbed back into bed with Zinzi after a scalding hot shower where I scrubbed my skin clean despite not having technically committed a sin tonight. Then I held her tight, didn't sleep at all and promised I'd never fucking let her go ever again.

When the news reached her that Ledger Raymond was dead over breakfast the next morning and she asked if I had a hand in it with questioning eyes, I kissed her hard, relieved that I didn't have to lie.

EPILOGUE TWO

FALCON - LOVE AND TOY

I watched Beau play with Sylvie in the common room for long enough with their dominance games that I was hard up for my own brat and toy—depending on who wanted the role that night.

Beau liked to be worshipped, that much was clear as he made Sylvie wait for him night after night on her knees, squirming when he played with her with his toes teasing between her legs while the other frat boys and myself watched on, or gently choking her with his cock while he deep throated her and held meetings, teasing the fuck out of everyone present with the sounds she made for him on demand.

I admired his control, and wanted to be a fly on

the wall in his room when he fucked her, wondering if he took her gently, though I doubted it. Rumor had it that he and Crush shared their girlfriends at a local club. I was keen to check the place out with Bella and Rose, but for tonight, I had a different game in mind.

"Take her inside my room and prep her," I'd told him earlier.

Rose and I were still at a learning point. Bella was the girl I loved beyond a doubt, and though we'd recently moved past a place of gentleness, Rose...he came from my father's mafia hangers on. But he knew my preferences and liked to play with us both. He'd kissed me the night I met Bella on my super yacht bearing the same name as my girlfriend, and I'd talked to her about inviting him into our circle. She'd agreed, excited to try anything that pleased me, it seemed and together the three of us...worked, for whatever reason.

I'd go with it until we didn't.

Tonight, Beau had Sylvie on display. Her cheeks colored as he toyed with her breasts publicly, and she moaned for him, slutting it up as she seemed to know he wanted, even if humiliation wasn't her thing. He gave her his thumb to suck on when it grew too much for her and she sighed, sinking into her submission. My cock hardened at the sight, and that was my cue to attend to my own submissive, waiting for me behind a locked door.

Unlike Beau, I didn't share with the rest of the team, only one I trusted, and I didn't want anyone else looking at Bella the way Rose and I did.

"Have a good evening." I murmured, setting my whiskey glass on a side table and vacated the room without another word.

I made my way up the stairs where Crush's door was shut. He and his girlfriend, Willow, were in her dorm room tonight, I guessed from the silence behind his door, and Dex and Zin were already passed out after a marathon session earlier while we all headed downstairs for their privacy.

A double knock on my door earned me a run of footsteps and soft voices. The lock clicked. I counted to five to let Rose setup whatever scene he wanted me to see when I walked in. The emaciated man who never seemed to put on weight no matter how much I tried to feed him liked to set up artistic scenes.

He also loved watching ballet and once danced before he fucked up one knee in his youth. Then drugs took him along the path of addiction, and he ended up as a messenger boy for my father, the Gianio mafia Don in Italy.

And now, he worked for me.

Tonight, he stood off to one side, his hands coiled around Bella's heart shaped face as he arched her backwards into his kiss. She balanced one knee on a chair, her pale lilac dress ripped violently down the front to expose most of her stomach, and one breast. He groped her until she mewled, her hips tilted up for him. His pants were undone, his already cock out as she reached back and returned the favor, fondling him until he hardened for her.

Then, as I watched, he held her by the top of her head, and pushed downward, pivoting her on her knees to engulf his cock in her mouth in a single flow of movement so sensual I swore that I could feel her hot saliva coat my own cock.

"Fuck," I muttered, barely shutting the door behind myself as she sank deep on his cock, taking him to the back of her throat.

I ignored my girlfriend and stared straight at the man who had orchestrated the scene, cupping his face between my hands and melded our mouths together. He moaned as I kissed him deeply, thrusting my tongue into his mouth and tasting her there.

"Please," he whispered, already unbuttoning my shirt as her hands worked at my pants, rubbing me to hardness though I was already there after their act. "We need you."

"Then suck." I waited long enough for Bella to loosen my belt then grabbed his hair and shoved him to his knees to join her on the floor at my feet.

One of them fished my cock out of my pants then their mouths were on me. My head tipped back enjoying the pleasure of two hot, wet mouths licking and sucking along the hard length of my cock. Precum beaded at the head and someone captured that, licking it away like a trophy.

I glanced down in time to see them sharing my precum in a kiss so heady I had to shift my stance wider to avoid from swaying. My hands reached for them, massaging their scalps as they kissed and licked me, sucking and fondling my cock and balls.

"Who is the toy tonight?" I whispered, barely able to speak as they played with me in tandem.

"Toy," Bella spoke first, claiming the right as she slithered out of her ruined dress and turned around to present her ass to me, holding herself open. "Please?"

"Love me tonight?" Rose leaned down to bite her

ass. "She insisted," he murmured when she whimpered and writhed for us both.

I raised an eyebrow, reaching for the lube on my nightstand. I hadn't done a lot of anal with Bella, but if that's what she wanted tonight, and I needed it rough, then that's what I would give her.

I startled when her cold hand closed on my outstretched wrist, so much closer than I expected.

"Sorry," she grinned at me, kissing my cheek.

"Very sorry." Rose's hand on my other wrist was equally cold, and clinked.

I looked down at both wrists, encircled with custom made titanium cuffs that I knew I wouldn't be getting out of any time soon, because I had used them on Rose several times.

"This is...different." I looked back at them, holding each gaze one at a time to register my curiosity at their actions. "Did you have a plan for afterward? Because I'll be fucking furious once you let me go."

"Maybe." Bella leaned down and nipped my earlobe with her teeth.

"You fucking little brat." I hissed air between my lips. "Give me that sassy mouth."

She kissed me hungrily as I requested, then

pulled back, only to sink down and suck my cock like she wanted to devour me.

"Fuck," I muttered, straining against the cuffs that refused to budge from where I had drilled the supporting chains into my heavy wooden bed posts. Dammit, I'd done a good enough job that they weren't budging. I was here until they let me out.

"May I?" Rose slid his hands under my half undone shirt and worked on my cuffs, then at my nod, slipped it off me. His hands brushed over my nipples.

He played there for a while, teasing me until I rested my head back against his shoulder. He sighed his pleasure at being allowed to touch me freely, and I smiled at the new knowledge, secreting it away.

My pants he pushed down to my knees, apparently not caring about comfort. I added that misdemeanor to his tally.

"Be careful what you do tonight," I murmured in warning.

He leaned in and licked across my bottom lip the same way I had the night I met him. "Don't worry, I have a plan," he whispered.

My cock pulsed in Bella's mouth, and she moaned, pulling off me. Her body turned and she impaled herself on my cock, working herself onto me until her peachy ass pressed to my thighs where I still knelt upright, my arms stretched out in a cross position. Bella rocked herself back and forth on my cock, moaning softly.

"I could have done this for you, Bella," I chided her.

"Mm, but this way, we get to fuck you as our toy." Rose picked up the lube, added a generous amount in his hand and shifted behind me. Cold fingers slid down my crack and I groaned my pleasure as he worked his fingertips into my asshole as Bella fucked herself gently onto my cock.

"Slow, gorgeous. Or I'll disgrace myself for you,." I murmured, gritting my teeth.

Rose reached around and flicked my nipples. "But your stamina is legendary. I wanted to test that out." One finger, then two, invaded my hole. He pumped my cock slowly, working me at the same rate as she did. Pleasure built as she fucked me gently, and I shuddered.

"This could be very fast," I muttered, unwilling to break the picture he had in his head but giving him a fresh dose of reality at the same time.

Rose laughed in delight. "Did you think we were going just once?" He kissed just below my ear as his fingers disappeared and more lube poured down my crack. "Deep breath," he mocked, using the same words I said to him on our first time and I knew he would be hard and brutal, just as I had been to him.

I closed my hands into fists. And smiled.

Brutal, I could survive.

He lodged his cock at my hole and pushed forward. I groaned my pain laced pleasure as he fucked me into her, willing myself to not come too fast. The feel of him inside me for the first time was exquisite. I gasped as I filled Bella too fast but Rose just laughed at my humiliation, reaching under me to grasp my balls and squeeze.

"You do need training up, don't you?" he mocked, stroking and fucking me at the same time.

I gasped, straining in my cuffs as my cock hardened impossibly. My orgasm stuck in my throat until I could barely breathe. Bella fucked herself on my hardening cock, moaning like a beautiful slut for us both.

And then I discovered what being fucked by Rose really meant. The artistic man had a sadistic streak as he slammed into me over and over. My ass was on fire as I cried out. He sucked on my neck, rubbing my balls and tugging on them every time I thought I might come, preventing the urge. My cock sprang back to life until we were jackhammering into Bella together.

When he finally let my balls go, I screamed through my orgasm, filling her with everything I had left and slumped forward in my chains.

Rose withdrew with the sort of tenderness I understood from the man, kissing all over me. He disappeared while Bella stayed with me. A moment later he returned, cleaning my body with a warm washcloth. Then they unchained me and wound us together, rubbing cream into the places that needed it on both of us.

"We wanted you to understand what it felt like to be our toy tonight." He held us both gently, Bella curled between us, and kissed me over her head. "How overwhelming and blissful it can be. Because I love being your toy, and I didn't want you to miss that, sir. I didn't know if maybe you might want to be our toy again, just sometimes," he offered hesitantly. "But also I understand if you need to punish me for taking your freedom."

He hung his head, and kissed the top of Bella's.

I watched them carefully, how he wrapped his body around hers, protective to the last. This had been her idea, not his and yet he risked me casting him out of our relationship when our love was the most tenuous at this point. Despite my burning asshole, I smiled.

"Yes, it was overwhelming, but it was also all the things you described. I would love to be your toy and to experiment, but on occasion, please," I murmured. "I might be a...good toy."

"I'd like that," Bella's voice came out of the middle of our melee, albeit muffled.

I reached between our bodies to squeeze her cheeks. "Of course you would, you little brat," I murmured fondly.

She snuggled in, and Rose leaned his head on top of hers, sighing when I kissed his lips, and let his eyes drift shut.

Falcon has his own book, SPRING BREAK WITH A MAFIA PRINCE

READ NEXT

I hope you loved Dex and Zinzi's story. Read on for a glimpse into Barclay's cheeky story in MY FAKE FRENCH MENAGE

TAILGATE

CHAPTER ONE - BARCLAY

BARCLAY

"Do you want to come on a date to a castle? Not a real one, just a fake one."

Those were the words that fell out of my mouth as I stared down at the prettiest little thing Rippton U had to offer.

Genie Lockwood.

Cute, sweet, and nothing like my fucked up mess of an ex.

And I screwed my chances with her the moment I ballsed up enough to ask her out.

But as always, Genie surprised me.

"The castle, or the date?" She tilted her heart shaped face up and pierced me with those burnt honey eyes that read the lies etched on my soul.

"I beg your pardon?" Twenty-one years of immaculate chevalier training kicked in and preserved my pasty ass.

"Barclay Augustus Chesterfield. Pay attention. Which one is the fake part? I mean, a crappy cardboard castle sounds terrible but a fake date I can do." She smiled brightly, though her eyes remained curious.

Now she thinks I'm a fucking loon.

Not that she'd be wrong.

I coughed into my fist, my cheeks heating as a pretty girl watched me with equally pretty eyes. "Uh, no. The castle is real."

"Awesome." She bounced a little on the balls of her feet and beamed at me. "Where are we going?"

"France?" I winced as her eyebrows rose. "I mean, that's where the family dinner is, and I need a date. It's about two hours west of Paris. And... I might have told my mother I had a plus one," I muttered, breaking eye contact and tried not to wince.

Fail.

Not my finest moment.

"Okay." She beamed at me, all cute and stunning and droolworthy.

I closed my mouth with a wet-sounding snap.

"You're coming?" I couldn't keep the surprise out of my tone.

"I mean, I'll be your fake date, Barclay." She shimmied her shoulders, that same cheeky glint in her eye. Wait. Was my crush *flirting* with me? "When is it?" She still had that curiosity over conflict expression, but rather than being shy like I expected, she looked more... excited.

I nodded like a fucking bobble head dog. "You know, I've had a crush on you for the last two years."

Two years I'd been at Rippton U where I enrolled my English-French noble ass to get the fuck out of Dodge...or at least the hell away from my responsibilities.

The elite private college seemed a good place to make new friends and discover fresh enemies and screw everything that walked past without regard to gender. Being away from France gave me the ultimate freedom, which I paid a hefty price tag for, though the multimillion dollar personal tithe all students paid barely scratched the surface of my bank account.

Genie laughed, a tinkling sound that turned every head in the courtyard. "Of course, I know you've been crushing on me, Barclay." She patted my arm. "The trip will be fun. When do we leave?"

"Tonight?" I raised both eyebrows. Asking about mundane things like clothes, packing, or passports never crossed my mind. Genie Lockwood was heiress to one of Europe's largest luxury brands. She probably travelled more than I did.

And just like me she was off boarded to Ripton U to learn a little American, uh, culture, and to make the connections with the other offspring of the ridiculously wealthy that would take her future empire higher.

She smiled and tossed her hair over her shoulder. "I think I can do that. France is quite lovely. See you when you pick me up."

When I expected her to turn away, she caught me in her piercing gaze again, raised up onto her toes, and brushed those plush, dusky pink lips across my cheek. A series of tingles sparkled across my shoulders and right to the base of my spine.

"Will do, " I managed to force out past dry lips, staring more like an American than the hybrid French–British marquess that I was.

Genie sashayed away, and my eyes fell to those luxurious hips with curves just large enough to fill my palms. I wanted to hold onto her and bang all night long like my life depended on it.

A few steps along her genteel retreat, she gave a little wiggle.

I stared.

Was that a happy dance?

I shook my head and headed back to the Kingsman's house, wondering why it was suddenly me who wasn't sure what the hell I got myself into, and not her.

"Not the armor again. Jesus wept, Barclay." Beau Bennett folded his arms and blocked my progress along the upstairs hallway of the Kingsman frat house.

The house where I lived for the past two years and left when an offer to get the hell out of the sights of this asshole came up. Beau Bennett was scarier than my grandmother on my English side, and that was saying something.

I straightened, tugging at the bowtie at my throat with one finger, and strangled the thick rope connected to the ancient chest scraping its way along the plush carpeting in my wake with the other.

Time to fess up.

"Okay, so my lazy ass didn't move all the armor

last time when I left, and I have to reclaim this. Plus, I'll get castrated by someone so much worse than you if I don't take it back." The concept of not returning to France without the entire contingent of family armor didn't bear thinking about.

Beau's eyes narrowed, and I became the sole focus of his attention. "Why?"

One word, and the man gave me whiplash.

I froze like a Rippton U goalie against an oncoming Blackstone U opposing team hellbent on our mutual destruction. The last time I flirted with him, Beau ended up with both the girls I wanted, fucking them publicly on party night. The whole debacle left me whimpering after my conniving ex and becoming involved with her again turned out to be a poor choice in a long line of equally shitty decisions.

I moved out of the Kingsman house to get the fuck away from Bennett and his ilk the following week, preferring the mixed odd company of the rockstar, the geek, the goth girl, and the tennis champion who made up my current household.

Along with the rest of the family armor.

Not taking the whole lot with me at the time seemed remiss at this point, but I hated sweating.

Just another fucking poor decision on the Bennett-Barclay train.

Which brought me back to the asshat blocking my path with broad shoulders and suck-me-off worthy lips.

"Move," I said tightly, flapping a hand at him.

"If I don't?" Beau's dark eyes glinted as he stared me down.

I'll find the Claymore and cut off your goddam balls.

My mouth kept mum on that one, thank fucking God. Otherwise, it would've been somebody else who got castrated. My mother wouldn't be pleased to miss out on doing it for me.

"Move." I shoved aside my exhaustion.

The Kingsman attic was dry, dusty and made up of fifteen feet and twelve steps of utter hell that no one but me ventured into for the past fifty years. Sweat trickled into the crevices in my elbows and along my back, itchy fingers trailing in a slow procession to the small of my back.

I straightened to my full height and planted my feet squarely, managing to stare him down, gaining half an inch on his height thanks to the stout heels on my Italian loafers.

Beau blinked. The corner of his mouth lifted in a fleeting smile. "That was... Cute."

My dick started to harden.

"Don't fucking flirt with me," I snapped. "Go play with some other goddamn lord, like Nelson. Besides, don't you have your own Toy?" I trotted on out his pet term for the girl he loved to fuck not so quietly around the house with the sort of showmanship that made him forget why he clung to her so tightly int he first place.

Beau Bennet wasn't half as untouchable as he thought.

One instant, a snarky remark, and all the humor left his face. "That wasn't smart."

I smirked, just to shit him further. "Probably not."

"*Barclay*," cried a soft voice I recognized from the way the asshole made her scream loud enough to ruin a good night's sleep for the entire household. Those cries on nights while I lay beside my ex-cum-girlfriend-turned-psycho left her voice utterly recognizable and me very damn lonely with my cock in my hand.

A dark head whipped out from behind Beau and darted toward me. Slender arms engulfed me at waist chest level, and the tiny woman hugged me with all the considerable strength she hid in a fun-sized package.

I rested one hand on her head, twirling the dark strands between my fingers. "How are you doing, chipmunk?"

Sylvie batted her lashes as she looked up at me, giggling. "I'm good." She snuggled for a moment longer then detached herself, glancing over her shoulder at Beau who glowered at both of us.

"If you're done." A muscle along his jaw flexed, his eyes blazing as he stared at her and then lifted his gaze to me.

Now that's some possessive alpha level shit.

I knew a man like that once. He'd been good fun to play with, for a single season back in France. The year I found I had a heart, despite my mother's efforts to the contrary.

I bent down to Sylvie's level, and just to shit Beau up the wall, I kept her chin in my hand and tipped her head back, so she was looking straight at me as I lowered my face to hers, like I might kiss her. "Be a good little Toy, and ask your boy to move for me, honey?"

A secondary use of all his little keywords that he didn't keep mum about around the house seemed warranted.

I might be poppish, petty even. Hell, I was born that way. But if Beau Bennett thought he had the market cornered on keeping house secrets, he had a long way to go. I was bred on intrigue in French courts, and learned the names of the current prince's seven secret mistresses while the eighth, and most recently discarded one, taught me how to make a woman orgasm in just as many ways the hour after she left the palace.

"Say bye-bye, Toy," Beau murmured, his voice lowering the easy words to a threat.

Sylvie rolled her eyes at him and winked at me. "Move, Beau." She stepped into him, resting her hands on his abdomen and sliding them down to drift across the top of his leather belt. "Don't we have other things to do?"

He swallowed, his hands cupping the back of her head, drawing her up onto her toes, so that he didn't have to bend down. "Don't test me, Toy. "

He only had eyes for her, and a pit of absolute nothingness opened up inside me for all sorts of the wrong reasons.

Taking the opportunity Sylvie granted me with her brand of distraction, I dragged my chest of armor around the soon to be snogging couple, and down the hall. The strain killed my shoulders, but I didn't stop, not until I made it to the top of the stairs. Only then did I glance back, just in time to see Beau back Sylvie into his room and had the pleasure of experiencing a secondhand moan not meant for me before he kicked the door shut.

My exodus out of the frat house was accompanied by the sort of music I wanted to play myself, rather than witness. My mind drifted to Genie and what might be—if we were lucky—awaited us in France.

Or what might not.

Who knew what a castle fake date weekend would bring?

Read Barclay's story in A ROYALLY FAKE FRENCH MANAGE here.

AUTHOR'S NOTE

As an Aussie, lots of my Aussieisms do make it into my stories, no matter how hard I try to push them back. These are not spelling errors. Sometimes, they are placed there by design. You'll find a few of them in with Dex, and Nelson is a great, albeit British device—sorry, character—who lips off at will. He is a fun mouthpiece where I get to add in the occasional slice of my own culture. Please forgive him for any out of character moments where I just couldn't help myself. 'Stunned mullet'—the ignominious face someone pulls when they're startled—and 'pissed as a parrot' —also comes under 'drunk as a skunk' gets regular use as well as appearing in Dex and Zinzi's story.

ABOUT THE AUTHOR

ABOUT THE AUTHOR

USA Today Bestselling author Sofia Aves writes fast-paced police romances, sizzling military units, steamy cowboys with a Montana backdrop and the occasional cheeky god. Sofia writes kidlit for charity and has over one hundred and fifty publications across five not-so-super-secret pen names. She's the acquisitions editor for Evernight and Evernight Teen publishing and is a mum of three crazies in a returned veteran household. Sofia has two overly large fur babies who think they're teacup puppies.

Sofia lives near Brisbane, Australia where she has her own alpaca park, Lorendel.

www.sofiaaves.com

Sign up to Sofia's newsletter and get a free Blue Blooded Brothers book.

Haven't read the Z Boy's prequel? Get it for free here:
A TABLE FOR TEN

READ SOFIA'S SERIES

Blue Blooded Brothers

Collision

Politics & Paperwork

Blindsided

Sentinel

Mugshots & Candy Canes

Impact

Reckoning

Red Hart Ranch

Snow on the Range

Siren on the Range

Sundown on the Range

Spirit on the Range

Ash on the Range (2025)

Mistletoe on the Range (2025)

Texan Devils
Ranger's Wish
Ranger Bedevilled
Ranger's Passion
Ranger's Fury
Ranger's Wrath
Ranger's Storm
Snapdragons & Seductions
Summer with a Ranger
Merry with a Ranger

Playing to Win
Off Boarding
Vicious Slash
Zero Pointer
Off Stage Fling

Rippton Allstars
Crushing It
Glacial Force

Rippton Creatives
Study Games
Make Me, Break Me

Twisted Obsession
Spring Break with a Mafia Prince
A Royally Fake French Menage

Jericho Chimeras
Puck Me Always
Puck My Heart
Puck me Sideways

Z Boys
King
Joker
Hearts
Ace
Mayhem & Mistletoe
Ruski

Fast Track to Love
Speed Trap

Klauss Brothers
Zander
Keegan

Gallo Empire *with Jade Marshall*
Splintered Vows

Fractured Vows

Fierce Vows

Savage Covenant

Rom Coms

She's A Hot Christmas Mess

Boats, Moats and Root Beer Floats

Writing Why Choose Dark Romance as

DOVE PRIEST

Recurve Ridge

Kidlit writing as

JO SEYSENER

The OCD Elf

writing YA as

JOSS PHOENIX

Alchem Academy (2025)

Writing spicy paranormal romance as

RAVEN HUSH

Club Fray

Darkest Desires

Purge

Kidnapped By Claws
Ruin

Shadow Lords
Sinner's End
Heaven's Gate (2026)

Monster Brides
Phoenix's Eternal Flame
Kraken's Vow
Krampus' Christmas Bride

Silent Sentinels Duet
Reflections of Silence
Echoes in the Void

Monsters In New York
Feral Moon Rising (2025)